THE WHITE RE

C000154268

24

CELINE

BEHRANG KARIMI AND ALASTAIR MACKINVEN
27 FEBRUARY – 31 MARCH 2019

MAUREEN PALEY, LONDON

MICHAELA EICHWALD
23 MARCH – 19 MAY 2019

MORENA DI LUNA, HOVE

MAUREEN PALEY
MORENA DI LUNA

21 HERALD STREET, LONDON E2 6JT
3 ADELAIDE CRESCENT, HOVE BN3 2JD

TELEPHONE +44(0)20 7729 4112
WWW.MAUREENPALEY.COM

Anthea Hamilton

The Prude

8 March - 18 May, 2019

THOMAS DANE GALLERY
3 & 11 Duke Street, St James's
London, SW1
www.thomasdanegallery.com

Your Blues Michael Schmelling   skinnerboox.com + theiceplant.cc

A Tale of Mother's Bones:
Grace Pailthorpe and Reuben Mednikoff
and the Birth of Psychorealism

12 April —
23 June 2019

Free admission
Camden Arts Centre
Arkwright Road
London NW3 6DG
camdenartscentre.org

ARTS COUNCIL
ENGLAND

Camden
arts centre

Reuben Mednikoff, March 20, 1936 – 1 (The Stairway to Paradise), 1936
The Murray Family Collection (UK and USA)

Sadler's Wells Theatre
sadlerswells.com
020 7863 8000
Ⓣ Angel

"Among the world's most elegant
and refined companies"
New York Times

29 May - 8 June

San
Francisco
Ballet

Helgi Tomasson, Artistic Director

Published by The White Review, March 2019
Edition of 1,800

Printed by Unicum, Tilburg
Typeset in Nouveau Blanche

ISBN No. 978-0-9957437-6-2

The White Review is a registered charity (number 1148690)

The White Review, 8–12 Creekside, London SE8 3DX
www.thewhitereview.org

Supported using public funding by
ARTS COUNCIL ENGLAND

EDITORIAL

In August 1915, *The Egoist* – an avant-garde magazine which claimed to 'recognise no taboos' and had serialised *A Portrait of the Artist as a Young Man* and *Ulysses* while James Joyce's work was banned – announced that it was launching a Poets' Translation Series. With translations from Greek, French, Italian, Russian, Spanish and Hebrew, it aimed to capture the history of European literature in a unified collection, and thus to keep a spirit of internationalism alive at a time of crisis. In 1941, as the continent was divided in another war, the Hogarth Press published a journal titled *Daylight*, a collaboration of English and Czech writers printed to 'reaffirm a belief that the culture of Europe is fundamentally one' and to establish an artistic alliance that would prove 'more valuable and more lasting than any political accommodation of the moment'. Over the period during and between the two world wars, little magazines – among them *Horizon, New Writing, Left Review, Criterion* and *Adam International Review* – looked to counter the tide of nationalism in Europe by forming new and unexpected alliances within their pages, by juxtaposing the work of British writers with their counterparts from other cultures, and by foregrounding translation as an act of solidarity. As we planned this issue of *The White Review*, knowing it would be published in the month that the UK is scheduled, at time of writing, to leave the European Union, we looked, in some small way, to their example, seeking to put together an issue concerned with language, understanding, and dialogue across borders – not only trans-European, but internationally.

This issue's roundtable takes as it subject translation. Our participants – Khairani Barokka, Rahul Bery, Kate Briggs and Jakob Stougaard-Nielsen – discuss 'fluency as power', language extinction and oral cultures, and making mistakes. A theme returned to throughout the discussion is translation's nature as essentially relational and collaborative: a practice, as Briggs puts it, that 'is attached to something else, and arrives pointing to something other than itself'. As if to show the theory in action, Adam Thirlwell's essay/journal offers an account of his process of translating a poem by his friend Alejandro Zambra, and is replete with distractions, memories and incidental observations as he ponders word-choice and subtext. Presented in conjunction with Zambra's poem, this collaboration is a moving meditation on the infinite misunderstandings that characterise human relationships.

'Letter-writing,' says Mary Ruefle, 'is my favourite genre, next to haiku'; we present here the record of the poet's year-long correspondence with our online editor Cecilia Tricker, which ranges over writing rituals, childhood and invisibility, and contains some of the wisest life-advice we've recently encountered. We're also delighted to present an interview with German novelist Jenny Erpenbeck, an unsettling story by the Man Booker International-shortlisted Argentine writer Ariana Harwicz, and debut fiction by Zakia Uddin, a deadpan exploration of love and manipulation at a provincial dance school. They are joined by an extract from a new novel by Egyptian writer Nael Eltoukhy, elegantly translated from the Arabic by Robin Moger. Set around the time of the 2011 revolution, the book traces its protagonist's disintegration into madness and murder against the backdrop of political upheaval. Elsewhere, Rebecca Tamás's luminous, spell-infused essay 'The Songs of Hecate' is both a manifesto for her own poetics and an interrogation of 'what it might be possible to make language do, what might be made possible through language'. Our cover is designed by the artist Anthea Hamilton, who is interviewed in this issue. Hamilton's work encapsulates a concern that seems to bind these pieces together: her playful, political, bold work explores, as Emily LaBarge writes, 'utopias and collectivity... attempts at finding a "shared language", or an alternative mode of existing within the world.'

THE SONGS OF HECATE: POETRY AND THE LANGUAGE OF THE OCCULT

REBECCA TAMÁS

I have gone out, a possessed witch,
haunting the black air, braver at night;
dreaming evil, I have done my hitch
over the plain houses, light by light:
lonely thing, twelve-fingered, out of mind.
— Anne Sexton

Above all, magic seemed a form of ... insubordination, and
an instrument of grassroots resistance to power.
— Silvia Federici

BEGINNING 1 (DISGUST)

This is the tower of the past. The battlements are formed of anthills, the
anthills the curves of the goddess, the curves snakes agreeing sealing
themselves away. Lookouts lie face down, mouths open to the earth,
swallowing the matter of their warnings.
— Nisha Ramayya

In the room full of witches, I am meant to be disgusted. Disgusted, or
scared, or even, perhaps, aroused. Each artist in the 2014 British Museum
exhibition *Witches and Wicked Bodies* hoped to elicit these reactions from
their images, which took the form of etchings, paintings, sketches; images,
without exception, of women. Some of the pictures show 'crones' or 'hags'
sketched with crude, banal misogyny: breasts drooping, private parts
rubbing against chapped broomsticks. Some have the veneer of seduction:
tempting sorceresses who hover over gently bubbling cauldrons, long
black hair slithering round tight waists, robes billowing in the silver
moonlight. Each image was designed by rigid Christian imaginations to
create fear, to create disapproval, horror or disgust – women copulating
mid-air under starlight; women worshipping at strange altars; women
tearing off the body parts of men; women carving runic images; women
dancing backwards on the Sabbath; women making love with dogs and
frogs and toads. Yet each one awakens me. These women are undoubt-
edly *BAD* and *EVIL* and *GROSS* and *DEGENERATE* and *UGLY* and
SEXY and *SHALLOW* and *PAINTED* and *OLD* and *YOUNG* and
HUNGRY and *MAD* and *DANGEROUS* and *AWFUL*. Yet I am not
disgusted. Instead I am deeply happy to be with them. I am happy because
of their power. When I got home, I wrote a poem – it was a spell.

BEGINNING 2 (HISTORY)

If you are a woman, writing about your experience of being a woman,
you are part of one of the most avant-garde literary movements there
has ever been.
— A.K. Blakemore

In recent years, in the UK, and across Europe and the US, there has
been a growing fascination with the occult, and especially with the
figure of the witch, in all her variety, difference and infinite capacity.
Much has already been written about contemporary Western culture's
renewed interest in witchcraft and the occult, from the appearance of
'insta-witches' to the rise of neo-pagan practice. But what I want to do

here is think about this 'occult moment' in relation to poetry. I want to explore this because these occult elements, to me, seem to offer something that speaks particularly to the nature of and difficulties of poetry itself – to what it might be possible to make language do, to what might be made possible through language. My particular occult interest is the witch – the witch as an explosively radical female figure, a site of resistance, a way out of silence and silencing. What she has made possible for me is a new relationship with poetic speaking, with the power of the word, and with what that power might make possible for liberatory, feminist thinking. But before I begin to unpick those possibilities, I need to look back.

Silvia Federici, historian, theorist and Marxist-Feminist activist, is a key thinker for establishing the figure of witch-as-resistance. In her 1998 book *Caliban and the Witch*, Federici writes about the European 'witch panics' or witch trials of the early sixteenth century, where approximately 60,000 people, most of them women, died. She questions the traditional historical narratives around these 'witch panics', exploring the witch trials not as examples of mass hysteria and superstition, but as instances of state-sanctioned female repression:

> The witch was not only the midwife, the woman who avoided maternity, or the beggar who eked out a living by stealing some wood or butter from her neighbours. She was also the loose, pro-miscuous woman – the prostitute or adulteress, and generally, the woman who exercised her sexuality outside the bonds of marriage and procreation... The witch was also the rebel woman who talked back, argued, swore, and did not cry under torture.

The qualities of disobedience and free-thinking Federici describes, that led women to be condemned as witches, are the very ones we must now claim and re-figure: taking the clichés of the badly behaved harlot and the hysterical wild-woman, and turning them over to reveal their power-ful and dissident underside. For Federici, the witch was a figure of anti-colonial, anti-Western resistance, who rejected state power and misogyny; a woman doing battle with the many manifestations of racist, patriarchal and hegemonic societal control.

The version of the witch that Federici is describing is one who emerges, imaginatively, through Western ideas of what a witch is – the demonic, malevolent figure of Christian mythology, re-figured as a force of liberation. This witch is always marginal, always despised, inevitably resistant. She is a mixture of myth and reality – of healers, midwives, 'good' witches and pagan priestesses, lumped together by the pious imag-inations surrounding them, which saw these innovative and powerful women as ungodly and profane; which took folklore and suspicion and branded it onto their bodies; which saw their strength – in whatever form it manifested – as evil, rather than fruitful.

In non-Western societies the picture is, and has been, very different. Certainly there have been witch trials across the world, and the perse-cution of 'witches' (most of these so-called witches would never define themselves as such) remains current, especially in The Democratic Republic of Congo and Ghana. But at the same time, once we step outside of Western hegemony we also awaken to the traditions where magical power has held real importance to the culture at large. In Southern African tradition the figure of the 'sangoma' is a diviner or fortune-teller, who seeks out illness or even predicts the future, while the 'inyanga' uses magic to heal illness and restore strength to her patients. In Mexico there has long existed an indigenous practice of brujería (witchcraft), Santería, voodoo, occultism and magic, explored by all genders. This witchcraft is such a part of ordinary life that despite Mexico's strong Catholicism, one can go to the *Mercado de Sonora* in Mexico City for magic herbs and occult supplies, as easily as you might get your groceries. In Diné Native American culture, 'witchcraft' itself is seen as a powerfully negative force, but spiritual leaders with magical abilities perform 'sings' for healing and the safety of

their community, harnessing occult power for good.

Whether used as a way to think through female power, queer sexuality, class insurrection or indigenous freedom, the witch can be a powerful figure of strength, sexual and emotional freedom and justice. But she is experienced and harnessed in many different ways within different communities, and through different intersections of oppression and experience. There is no one witchcraft, and there is no one witch. I listen and learn, and consider my version of the witch as only one small part of a powerful, diverse and vibrant world of expression. My own witchcraft does not begin with my ancestors, or with my individual history – my witchcraft begins, and lives, in language, and what language might make possible; how it might turn our fury, and our knowledge and our desire, out into the teeming world through the mouth of a poem.

ANGER

I have not been able to touch the destruction
within me.
But unless I learn to use
the difference between poetry and rhetoric
my power too will run corrupt as poisonous mold
or lie limp and useless as an unconnected wire
– Audre Lorde

Where do I look for all the angry women's voices? Where do I look for all the really angry women in writing, in art? After all, I am so angry. I do not find that a rare or unusual state.

Sara Ahmed talks of the importance of being a 'feminist killjoy', of bringing 'negative' aspects of patriarchy and racism into the light. Being a feminist killjoy means being prepared to be 'the cause of bad feeling', and being 'willing' to create this bad feeling; remaining angry, despite the inevitable criticism and repression, 'because that's a sensible response to what is wrong.' Anger is, then, a *necessary* response to our situations, a proportional reaction to our complicated history and our present moment. It is also powerful in its disrupting and upsetting potential – not bending ourselves to patriarchal expectation, but resisting, whatever we might then be called in retaliation. Anger is the cause and the tool of feminist uprising and change, the energy that pushes up from the ground of the past and into present possibility. Thus, anger is often a crucial part of feminist or liberatory poetics: poetics that seeks to use language as a space for transformation and change.

How then to build a truly convincing, and new, *angry* language in poetry? One that reveals and makes change without destroying, undermining or silencing the expresser of that anger? There are many ways, of course, but one thing I keep returning to in my store of resources, relatively ignored by patriarchal capitalism, are hexes. Spells. Curses.

Rituals. The language of undoing, of hate that *does something*, that doesn't rebound on its owner and turn her to ash, but names and recognises the hurt, purges it and makes it ashamed.

The witch's anger can be cold (considered, vengeful, clever) or hot (thick, vibrant, cleansing, furious) but in either form it is she who is in control, she who decides how to channel and use it. For a witch, anger makes things happen. It is creative, relaxing, rich. No personal destruction. No apologies or reticence or politeness. The witch absorbs anger as an inherent part of her self and her life force. She has no need to reject it as a dangerous emotion; instead it feeds her, makes her stronger. For anger to be a revolutionary force in thinking, it must be channeled; it must not collapse. In a society where, again and again, we see established forms of power fail vulnerable, oppressed or abused women, to serve the interests of powerful men, there is something particularly compelling, for me, about witches' angry magic.

The language of spells and hexes offers a powerful vector of movement, of becoming – one that allows the internal to become external, hate and anger to exit the victim and move outwards, giving relief, restoring agency, allowing feeling to become language, language to become action. This action is a refusal to shut up. It is a way of repeating the very things which patriarchal society would like to forget, and it is also a release – why should we shut up, just because it embarrasses people? Makes them uncomfortable? What if we take our spite and horror and pour them into language – make them a power source, not a drain? Poetry, like all kinds of language, has long been the preserve of powerful men. So spells, hexes and curses can offer renewed ways for a poet to write in a language that has not always had a home for her – shuddering and changing it so that she may inhabit it with more comfort, so that she may find ways to bend it into expressing what has long been muted.

Such use of the occult to channel anger, to protect and strengthen the silenced, does not exist only in poetry, but in the material organisation of many magical practitioners. We think of Tituba, an enslaved woman accused of witchcraft in the Salem Witch Trials. Tituba was caught up in a wave of persecution that sought to configure her indigenous practice as devil worship – a history of oppression which makes it unsurprising that African-American magic often focuses on protection and the restoration of community power, and the powerful inscription and expansion of ancestral and indigenous strength. In a modern context, 'Witches Against Trump', a global coven of contemporary witches, has come together over the internet to hex the president, an act that is both material and symbolic – restoring linguistic power to women, through the hexing of a man who often corrupts and maims language to reflect his own corrupt and misogynist agenda. The hexes on Trump rebut the idea that feminist movements such as #MeToo are 'witch hunts' in the traditional sense of the powerful hunting the powerless. Rather, as Lindy West wrote in her *New York Times* article about Woody Allen and Harvey Weinstein: 'Yes, This Is a Witch Hunt. I'm a Witch and I'm Hunting You.' In this version of the witch hunt, the witches are turning on misogynists in power and refusing to be subsumed or silenced. They are reversing the expected discourse and speaking back through spells and enchantments. These witches are not only finding new forms of expression, but are building female-identified solidarity across borders and nations through shared, and angry, magical language.

When a new friend or colleague says to me: *You're nice! You aren't scary at all, like I thought you would be from reading your poems*, I know the angry magic has worked. In a witch's hands, poetry's force of language becomes supple and wet: it circles round the silent void of women's history, like a damp finger round the rim of a glass, and you can hear something.

spell for joy

THESUN THESUN THESUN

nothing can be trusted!
raise up your rinsed hands!
terrible fury and becoming!
take off your clothes!

one colossal owner of the void
brightness folding into itself
again and again vulval or filo

I see a shaking which is total and absolute fear

one day yr gonna die!

the hot impossible apple of
your perfection

you freckled you covered in something
you utter

just open up your face
light's ice cream cone coming
on the inside of yr eyelids

say yes five thousand times
(o love)

TRANSFORMATION

I like when you rub sage on my door
I like the lamb's blood you throw on my face
I like heaping sugar in a jar and saying a prayer
And then having it work
— Dorothea Lasky

I was once interviewed for a university job (without realising who I was speaking to) by an expert of Western witchcraft and paganism, the historian Ronald Hutton. He had looked at a few of my poems and asked me, among various questions about pedagogical strategy and research frameworks, how I would define a witch. I said I would define a witch as someone who uses language to cause change in the material world. When we spoke later, Hutton told me that, though I didn't get the job, I had given him one of the best definitions of 'witch' he had ever heard. My feelings at that comment pretty much wiped out any disappointment about the job.

This small anecdote made its way into the 2017 book *small white monkeys* by the poet Sophie Collins. The launch of this book centred around the idea of shame. The poet Vahni Capildeo read a long poem which, in one section, described her having a conversation with a powerful poetry editor who had requested to meet her. Despite having invited *her*, the editor took their meeting as an opportunity to tell her that she was an utterly worthless writer, and should stop publishing. He poured out his barely concealed racism and misogyny directly to her face. He said all this while her book of poetry, which she had brought as a gift for him, sat in front of him on the table. Capildeo described how, in this moment of total horror, and shame, and attack, she suddenly felt the ghosts of Sylvia Plath and Virginia Woolf standing next to her, one at each side. With those writers close to her, ghosts pressing her body, she said, she lost her shame, came back to herself, and found it possible to take back her book from the publisher (to his horror and upset – after all, he was just trying to be 'helpful'), and leave.

Capildeo described these events as experience, rather than imagination or fantasy. They were something that had happened; a summoning. Unlike a spell, which uses language to create change, a summoning brings others into presence even when language has been temporarily lost. A summoning is the magical action of community – the awareness that what cannot be borne alone might be borne together. When Capildeo described her experience, in powerful poetic language, she widened that community further, including us, taking us into the fold. This was no kind of comfy, heartwarming community spirit, which ignores structural racism and misogyny in a kind of holistic fakeness; rather it was an injunction to join the poet in the moment of enforced shame and the moment of its undoing.

Capildeo's 'taking in' involved no merging – after all, the oppressions she experienced were particular to her position not only as a woman, but as a woman of colour. I cannot simply 'join in' with that oppression and 'share the load'. What Capildeo made possible, in her poetry, was a standing-with, a being-with, in which one is confronted by the complicated reality of her experience and the reality of the change that she brought about – both for herself and for her listeners, changed by what they heard. If we have to live with a history of silenced, damaged, unwell, suppressed women writers, Capildeo seemed to suggest, then we can at least work with that history, summon it into new, dynamic positions. This is not quite 're-writing' the past, because it is more potent than that. We can't change what has come before, but we can access it, and address it, differently – finding the power in creative female figures such as Woolf and Plath, rather than the tragedy and poignancy that they are often made to represent. This is not to ignore their suffering, but rather to locate the other parts of what they make available to us, their bravery, their intelligence and their fight. As the mystic philosopher Walter Benjamin wrote, 'Nothing that has happened should be regarded as lost for history.' History only finds a temporal existence in its contemporary expressions, and so when we change it, the change is real.

Capildeo confronted us with the knowledge that the past is not dead if we can bewitch its corpse in language and bring it back to us, hold its clammy, tender body in our hands; that fury can live and do its work like cleansing fire, magic that makes change, around and within language, and out into the world.

burn the fire and jump

dear heart

under all this is a centre of human jam
red and pulsing

what you feel touch your face
  in a wavering immense cut

the sun is hovering at her absolute mid-point

  do you feel that fucked and desperate gilding stir in you?

  your stinking consecrated jam?

  throw yourself down on the floor like a bad dog

get on your knees   and lick the boards

  get up again

the fire is doing things to you

 that feel amazing

this earth is so

        remarkable

MYSTERY

It was not my body, not a woman's body, it was the body of us all.
It walked out of the light.
— Anne Carson

Poetry, like the occult, embraces the necessary irrationality that exists
squashed up against rationality in the material world. It does not 'reject'
the rational, but it does extract what else is there, the elements that don't
fit. Dorothea Lasky, in her poem 'Thing', says, 'It is the irrational / That
is worth living for.' Irrationality is not apolitical, but politically radical;
radical because it takes an interest in what it's actually *like* to be alive as
a human being – what it's like to live alongside many nonhuman creatures
and things, what it's like to not make perfect sense, to not always be in
control of what happens, to want joy, to have a complicated body, to rise
and fall unpredictably, widely, to love or desire others more than 'pro-
creation' or 'hormones' ask of you, to want to worship while also feeling
extremely sceptical.

At an event where the American queer astrologer Chani Nicholas was speaking, a member of the audience asked (rhetorically) 'Why is it that all straight white men hate astrology?' Ignoring the slight exaggeration for effect (of course *some* straight white men love astrology, just not many), this struck me as an interesting enquiry. There are many elements to what might look like an answer. It can certainly be frustrating to get caught in the binary of male knowledge: rationality, science, facts; female/queer knowledge: irrationality, magic, feeling, instinct. After all, women and queer people are as capable of rationality as anyone else. Yet it is in the derided 'feminine' spaces of magic, myth, history and feeling that we have found new kinds of power, forms of knowledge that fill in the gaping wounds that rational capitalist society leaves in our communities and beings.

To assert that you like or believe in astrology, or tarot, or magic means asserting forms of knowledge which you cannot prove, whatever their importance to your life. But such fluid, unprovable understandings are not simply escapes from rationality. They are ways of challenging what power and knowledge are and might be, and asserting that there might be spaces in which emotion and feeling are valid forms of knowing; forms which can encompass a diverse female experience at odds with the structures that attempt to control us.

The poet, astrologer and cultural diviner Ariana Reines, talking to me over email about the huge recent growth in 'internet astrology', stated:

> I love that the internet loves astrology. I think this is phase one of the feminisation of this very warped and weird network. Astrology answers our yearning to feel more connected to the planet we live in and to the tiny corner of the cosmos that we occupy. I think the current craze for it is as much about the mass hangover from the old systems of knowing, which as everyone can see and feel, have made a hellhole of our strange and blue little home.

We live on a planet. We are part of a complex machinery orbiting a star in a universe of stars. For me, astrology is just one dimension of a much larger coming-to-consciousness that is beginning all around us while the most virulent forms of evil double down and metastasise.

Feminisation, for Reines, is not about any of the degraded associations of 'weakness' or 'shallowness' that stick to ideas of femininity like barnacles. It is not the decried 'feminisation' of late capitalism, where pundits bemoan the increase of 'female' jobs such as care work and retail work, as opposed to the more 'manly' pursuits of factory jobs and physical work – a world of emotional labour that will implicitly taint the action of masculinity. For Reines, feminisation, in this case through astrology, is a way of re-seeing the world, of removing the mental shackles that make 'rational' Western capitalism seem like a normal and logical system of living. In the case of Reines's astrology, knowledge is both inherently mysterious and hugely fruitful, deepening material understanding about other people and the world, at the same time as accepting forms of knowing that cannot be directly communicated. In this kind of thinking, what we learn from the occult is not the answer to questions, but ways to ask new questions.

Louis MacNeice, from his poem 'Snow':

> On the tongue on the eyes on the ears in the palms of one's hands
> There is more than glass between the snow and the huge roses.

The question this poem is asking is, what is that *more*? I don't *know* what happens in, between and around the glinting membrane of the world, the spaces of snow, of glass, of roses, but my body and my mind tell me that there are inhuman voices, light leaking through in shards, the smell of sun and plant matter. I know that's not it, but that it may be part of it. I know it's possible for me to *know* what's there, without ever being able to express it, in language, or even to myself.

If I had a simple kind of self-respect I would keep quiet about that thing I *know*. It would be easier: I wouldn't have to worry that people reading this might be embarrassed to read my poetry in the future. I would avoid raising something that is hard to talk about, because its paradoxes and subtleties are more fitted to the language of poetry: language that can hold knowledge and unknowing in balance, that can use language to go outside of the meanings language allows. I know it's a risk to mention it here because, even among the most supportive and thoughtful friends in the world, it can be hard to say the word *sacred*. The tender, gauche, fragile, unclear, freighted nature of this word makes it hard to bring into the open.

'Spirituality', when it is derided and taken advantage of in the West, when it is appropriated from indigenous cultures and diluted, turns the material strength and power of the sacred into the softness of catchphrases and distraction; be it some thoughtless yoga classes usurping ancient South Asian religious practices for improved toning, or those selling products like decorated scented candles and inspirational posters which proclaim self-care but make no effort to explore the societal conditions that make this care necessary. But the sacred – that mysterious, shifting, vital thing – should be accessible to anyone with an interest in the vibrant possibilities of material existence. The sacred, for me, is the strange holiness of being alive in a world of living things, the infinite possibilities for becoming, change, transformation and connection which that world offers. I want to be able to look for this mystery without being forced to name it, without having that sacred potential turned into mollifying and commodifiable products or systems.

I find, then, that I can most effectively get closer to kinds of sacred mystery in poetry's open expanses, rather than within a single form of religion, with its specific strictures, and expectations. Because in poetry, this sacredness, in all its lambent impossibility, can rush in. The play of language can crack it open like a dark blue egg, dribbling liquid you cannot explain, but want desperately to touch with the tips of your fingers.

Poetry can be frustrating because it doesn't always make sense, or have narratives we can follow. As hard as this can be, this resistance of linear meaning, of clarity, of A to B, also makes it the perfect vehicle for things which do not make total sense, which are not clear, which do not follow a plan. Poetry knows that expressions in language can be much more than the sum of their words – I can 'describe' a poem to you, its events, tone, style, rhythm, but until you read or hear it you have absolutely no idea what it is or where it can take you. The language *is* the meaning, *is* the experience. The sacred, too, is frustrating, because it can also not be explained in any way other than itself – it asks us for experience *as* knowledge, inside the body, specific yet impossible to pin down. Poetry is language that means in this way, that makes experience the source of meaning, rather than a route to that meaning.

Poetry brings what is hidden, what is beyond or outside of words, momentarily into language, through the complication of placing ideas and images next to each other, without them having to find total conceptual

or narrative clarity. In poetry things are glimpsed, touched, but rarely
held still – they remain a tangled, gloopy, struggling mess, and yet you
still might find something in them. Because of this, poetry is the perfect
place for the hidden to dip into view, to be witnessed without being
contained. This is not magic tricks, just magic: things unfixed and
hard to fathom and viscerally there. The mystery.

spell for reality

what do you do when the answer to
too much is absolutely nothing?
honey sits on the table
fat and glowing
winter light gives you a pass
nine minutes of feeling nearly
completely alive

sometimes the ashy body in the ground seems
to have all the answers
ultimate realness   nasty truth as the final only truth
why then   this stupid relentless yearning for snow
   why the honey and talking

the burning bush is another form of ultimate realness
but what is it telling us
certainly it's nasty
however also   gold
also the entire pocket cosmos shifting and flapping
gentle limbs   holding each other   in the depth of the fire

then   somehow

as much snow as you could ask for

wet-gold honey and locusts

RITUAL

war is corny & revolution threatens
irony, still I want my soft sockets
touched & refuse to give birth
heartlessly: I won't budge on wanting love:
human touch: not everything
has to be profitable
— Jenny Zhang

In an interview with *The Huffington Post*, the American queer poet and
seer-witch CA Conrad says:

> (Soma)tic poetry rituals create an extreme present, keeping us
> in the deep awareness of everything around us, a present tense

we didn't know we longed for until we find it … The magic of language is always counting on us to make the effort to reach it, and once we get there the real possibilities, the infinite possible directions are finally clear.

Conrad created (soma)tic poetry rituals to make creativity possible in an impossible situation: the aftermath of the homophobic murder of his partner, Earth. Conrad's (soma)tic poetry uses rituals and actions in the material world to produce language. 'My idea for a (Soma)tic Poetics,' he writes, 'is a poetry which investigates that seemingly infinite space between body and spirit by using nearly any possible THING around or of the body to channel the body out and/or in toward spirit with deliberate and sustained concentration. The writing of (Soma)tics is an engagement with the thing of things and the spirit of things.'

Conrad uses the ritual of repeated actions and language forms, interventions within 'normal' society, and connections with nature and mystic structure, for example, immersing himself in one colour all day, wearing it, eating it, keeping it near; being directed to write poetry by words taken at random from wildly different genres of books in the library, or following an ant back to its nest in the Chihuahuan Desert.

In enacting these focused rituals, Conrad manages both to write brilliant poetry, and deal with some of the pain and despair of traumatising events. These rituals belong to Conrad alone, and to his power and suffering, but they can show us a way into thinking about what it might mean to see language, to see poetry, as a direct reckoning with the world – a form of bringing ourselves into the present. In the same interview Conrad says:

> When I conduct (Soma)tic poetry workshops, especially in the university setting, there is often one or two young people who admit to feeling like they are wasting their time learning poetry or art while the world falls apart. One of my most important goals is to address THAT whenever it comes up, to make clear just HOW ESSENTIAL being creative is to the future health and happiness of our species and other creatures and plants.

Artistic creativity can seem like... what? Distraction? There are certainly forms of creativity that bury their head in the sand. But making art can also be a way of bringing the world to itself. In poetic language there is the capability to exist in a moment that is meaningful, yet without a clear takeaway message or 'value'. How strange. What is meaningful is not always straightforwardly 'useful' or 'productive'. To express it crudely, capitalism wants everything to have a value that can be fixed, and which is therefore commodifiable. If a poem does not tell us how to live morally, or how to 'get over' our problems, if it does not comfort or clearly 'entertain us', then what is it doing? Perhaps it might just be showing us something of the world covered over by familiarity – the differing, complicated world which we live in and have a right to witness, and become intimate with, and consider.

The poetic moment rushes at us, real and opaque and present; full not only of us, but of many other human and nonhuman beings and things. It is this *complexity* that we might be able to touch, just briefly, so that it isn't just us in a stifling prison of subjectivity, fixed eternally on purpose and result. The poem, in these cases, doesn't 'tell us something', it *is* something. The poem itself is a part of the world and its mystery and strangeness, and a passage into that world. It is part of the conflicting and varying forms of meaning and being that exist within it; ones that can never fully remain in our grasp, but which we can experience.

Wallace Stevens, from his poem 'The Snowman':

> For the listener, who listens in the snow,
> And, nothing himself, beholds
> Nothing that is not there and the nothing that is.

In this poem, the human witness of the world sees 'nothing that is', because he always brings himself, his imperfect understanding and conceptions to his seeing. Yet he also beholds 'Nothing that is not there'. He is blocked from seeing truly, at the same time that he sees everything – it is all in front of him, all real and materially present and full of its own agency, if he could find a way through himself to its reality.

It is the realisation of not knowing that allows us to momentarily glimpse the very reality of the world – what we don't know swimming into view in all its opaque, contained brightness. The poem becomes a form of ritual in which the present floods into our consciousness, full of evasive potential. This is poetry that gives us unexchangeable, unconsumable, resistant, vibrant knowledge: an occult practice of reality.

spell for emotions

make a cake that looks like a picture of your mother making a cake
set up an industrial skyline with more and more tender phalluses
hitting the air

don't   you realise   how little   time there is?

you can't set up a portfolio

or reason about the amount of passengers through the border

YOU HAVE TO START CRYING OR WHATEVER!

you have to cup a breast just there in the suggestive lamplight
or put yr mouth on a fox's mouth though it hurts and hurts
or carry a person on your back over a revered mountain

you have to

hurry hurry hurry hurry

& there are places in which love reproduces itself like a lizard's tail, heeds
to no alarm or database. places where the sun raises like a fat cunt
glowing in the sky.
— Sophie Robinson

In *Malleus Maleficarum* (often translated into English as 'The Hammer
of Witches') the fifteenth-century Catholic clergyman Heinrich Kramer
expressed his virulently misogynistic and vile thoughts on witchcraft,
encouraging rulers to hunt witches down, and to treat their crimes with
the same violence meted out to heretics – burning at the stake. Yet in
Kramer's text we can piece together the pieces of historical folklore, myth
and rumour which fed into the version of witchcraft believed at the time,
and turn them to our own devices. Kramer writes:

> [W]hat shall we think about those witches who somehow take
> members in large numbers – twenty or thirty – and shut them up
> together in a birds' nest or some box, where they move about like
> living members, eating oats or other feed? This has been seen by
> many and is a matter of common talk.

Apparently, a man who had his member taken by a witch was encouraged
by her, in reparation, to 'climb a particular tree where there was a nest
containing many members, and allowed to take any one he liked'.

Kramer existed in a world full of stories of penises in nests, fed and
watered, penises taken and returned, used for pleasure, penises put on,
worn, discarded, picked up again, exchanged, rejected. Kramer's world
also told of witches' vulva trees, couples copulating under them furiously,
vulvas fluttering open and closed like the wings of huge coloured butterflies. Kramer himself was disgusted and terrified by this bodily movement
and undoing, this fever of change, female power, and pleasure.

Yet Kramer's descriptions of fear and disgust at women's potential
agency and sexuality, can, like the etchings of witches' terrifying but vital
power, give us paradoxical insights into our own creative and political
needs. Kramer's book, and the stories of freeing sexual flexibility kernelled
within, help me to ask: how to find the magic of the body? How to bring
it into language?

Witches reach out and pluck from the branches exactly what their
bodies need. They do not worry about propriety, or fret about fixed shape
or the shape of others. They do not worry about the limits and expectations of their own desires. They do not worry about the material reality
of the body, its visceral need for sustenance and touch and increase, but
embrace that vitality and that extension. They reach out and take.

The witch does not find it hard or problematic to say cunt, or to have
one or not, or to interact with one. The witch eats onion rings, and fucks
with her hands still smelling of oil, turns into a dog, a wolf, a beast and
back again, and shifts, and laughs, and is happy. It is impossible to imagine
a witch faking an orgasm, or dieting to make herself manageable, or
putting up with boring or painful sex out of politeness or kindness, or
deifying penetrative intercourse, or tying sex to making babies, or accepting the construct of a virginity.

If to be human means being tied into a system of patriarchal power
struggle and rigidly heterosexual, normative sexuality, then the witch
will go beyond the human: slipping out of her skin into a body that shifts

and changes at each point of touching. The witch's sexuality gives her pleasure, but that is not all it gives her – it gives her material entry into the validity of her wants, the ability to love herself for her wishes and needs and longings. A witch's desire changes what is thinkable within the body – much like poetry might do.

The witch gets bigger and bigger and bigger. She shouts.

spell for the witch's hammer

a two pronged sword
to put them down

out there a lot of things happen

witches
undo each other   a candle in each opening

witches wake at night and cry
beasts with curly horns comfort them
/suck gently

witches go astray
carnality   swooping and fluttering like a ragged flag

they   laugh so much
covered in purple bruises
teaching tricks   GPS of the eternal flagellant light   always going home

the witch's hammer sinks into flesh
then   disappears   and only mercury remains   its little peasant trail

the witches eat your book
then you
then everything

JENNY ERPENBECK   INTERVIEW

Jenny Erpenbeck puts her finger where it hurts. Her writing career, now almost in its third decade, includes five novels, a book of short stories and a number of other publications, most of them translated into English by Susan Bernofsky. Throughout it all, she has examined the effects that political and societal systems have on the individual – whether the military dictatorship in Argentina in *Book of Words*, various European totalitarian systems in *The End of Days*, or the deadening bureaucracy of the contemporary German state in *Go Went Gone*, a deeply political novel longlisted (but not shortlisted) for the 2018 Man Booker International Prize.

We meet in Berlin, where Erpenbeck grew up on the GDR-side of the Berlin Wall, and where summer is drawing to a close as we talk in her study. It is a room filled with books, some of them her own: boxes of paperbacks, shelves and shelves of novels, monographs, history. Between them stands a beautiful model of a house – the country house on which *Visitation* centres – and a picture of her grandmother, the central figure of *The End of Days*, the novel that won her the 2015 International Foreign Fiction Prize and consolidated her reputation both in the English-speaking world and at home. Much of our conversation circles back to two topics that have occupied Erpenbeck throughout her career. First, there is recent German history, and in particular the GDR and its lasting effects. And then there are the themes of her latest book, *Go Went Gone*, a novel about a retired professor who becomes deeply involved in the lives of a group of refugees housed near his home – much like Erpenbeck herself, who drew on friends' lives for her protagonists. It is a novel that showcases Erpenbeck's deep concern with society as a whole, as well as her lucid understanding of the failures of the individual.

Throughout our conversation, we keep coming back to politics. It is the summer of 2018, and it would be impossible not to. It is a time when Erpenbeck's clear, sharp, always innovative prose feels like a gift, when her novels' cool assessing gaze and constant undercurrent of empathy and compassion feel miraculous.   THEODORA DANEK

TWR You grew up next to the Berlin Wall – quite literally. What was it like growing up with a border at the end of your street?

JE Well, I always say – and it often shocks people – that I had a happy childhood. Behind the Berlin Wall, where, supposedly, things were always grey and a Stasi man lurked behind every tree, you could have a happy childhood. As a child you accept everything at face value. You don't think about the Wall. And no matter how absurd the situation might have been – especially in the Leipziger Straße, where I could see the wall from our flat and even from our schoolyard – you take things as they come. I spent most of my childhood in the Leipziger Straße, and summers in the house that is at the centre of my novel *Visitation*. That was wonderful – as you can tell from that book, nature has been a constant in my life. Anyway, I was completely convinced that the Wall would be down when I reached adulthood.

I did have a privileged grandmother of course. She was a writer and worked for eight hours a day. She survived twelve years of fascism in exile, that wasn't easy – not just because she was in exile, but because surviving under Stalin was down to luck. I do think that, even though she was privileged in the GDR, her privilege was different from how, for example, a dentist is privileged.

TWR I often think about different types of privilege: money can be privilege, but so can education.

JE Education is really tied up with wealth nowadays. We do have to question, in Germany, whether we want a system like in America or England, where it is very hard for state schools to keep up with private schools due to the lack of public funds. Or if we try to keep the level that we have in state schools in Germany by supporting them, and sending our children to state schools. The support and structural prerequisites have to be provided by the state.

TWR What about your education?

JE Many things that we were taught in school were exactly the opposite of what people in East Germany now proclaim, for example when it comes to xenophobia. We learned about solidarity, especially solidarity with those without rights or privileges, and friendship between different peoples. I actually went to school twice: for my first book (*The Old Child*) I pretended to be ten years younger than I actually was. I went back to school

and repeated Year 11. That's how I got an insight into what school was like in the East, and what it was like in the West. To be honest I found everything incredibly easy the second time around.

TWR Your first two novels, *The Old Child* and *The Book of Words*, are both about children. Why?

JE Well, they're not really children. One of them is an adult who pretends to be a child, the other one is an adult who looks back on her life. I didn't think about it in a programmatic sense. The first story, for my debut novel *The Old Child*, was based on a real case [of an adult pretending they were a child]. And *The Book of Words* is based on a story from Argentina, where there were many similar cases [of children being taken away from their parents during the military dictatorship]. What I was interested in was this: as an adult you know more than as a child. When you look back and observe it all with the knowledge of an adult, you see what you may not have seen back then, and vice versa. As a child you also have a certain amount of good naiveté. You look at the world without preconceived notions. Similarly, when you write, you have to try to forget your prejudices and look at things as if it was the first time. I was intrigued by that, because you have at least two time periods, two levels of reality and perception piled on top of each other.

In *The Book of Words* I investigated the vocabulary, the stories that were told, plus the knowledge that the protagonist has come to since. With that, each word acquires a kind of space. Childhood is the time when identity is founded. That is when you are shaped forever. I was interested in exploring what you learn then, and how you learn things that make you say 'I'. It's so easy to say, 'I like this! I don't like that! That guy is an idiot!' – but then you look back and wonder, where did that actually come from? What shaped me in such a profound way that I can now say this sentence?

TWR So these novels are an attempt to deal with the memory of childhood?

JE Yes, or the attempt to stage a childhood – like my protagonist in *The Old Child* does. In many ways, childhood is a complex issue. When the GDR fell apart, people often said, 'We want to be responsible adults now. We don't want to be treated like children anymore.' The state arranged many things for you, and it did feel like a parent-child relationship. The old comrades thought they knew how to manage it all, it had an educational feel. That is another reason why the topic of childhood is so interesting – it's what the 'old child' from *The Old Child* likes: she's in a children's home, a closed-off society. She's safe there. It's a way of getting away from gender relations, too. The child also escapes from competition, from the rat race – adulthood is so often a fight for survival. Competition is very draining.

TWR   In the late 1990s you left Berlin and moved to Austria, where you worked in theatre. Did you notice the rise of the far right at the time? Did that shape your thinking?
JE   Not really. I worked at the opera house in Graz in Austria. For me, Austria was the South. I felt as if I had emigrated away from politics, from the endless debate about East and West. I didn't see the rise of the far right coming at all. At first it only seemed confined to the Eastern Bloc...

TWR   ...and now it's everywhere.
JE   That leads me to ask many questions. For example: Does humanity need a war every fifty years? After all, nationalism doesn't mean that everyone is good friends with everyone else, nationalism always ends in war. That has always been the case. It's probably a reaction to globalisation, because I do think that people find it hard to deal with the fact that the world has suddenly come so close. There's a discrepancy between the world that you perceive when you go shopping, when you drop your child off at school, and that of faraway countries. It's hard to make a connection between these two. Nationalism is a yearning for something. And that brings us back to the Wall. The Wall made it impossible to travel, and that was a shame. But it also meant that everyone was close together, everyone knew each other. It was like a nest – with Stasi agents. The world was readily comprehensible. That has now gone, and is hard to deal with. Nationalism isn't a solution, on the contrary, the world won't be more peaceful and the refugees won't disappear. But I can see the fears that cause it.

TWR   I guess that brings us to the question of home: what is seen as home, as familiar. The way that you describe the GDR makes it sound like a bubble.
JE   Yes, but there was also a general idea that there would be an evolution towards a more just world, and that would be progress. This idea of a direction, of progress, is completely gone now – and I don't mean progress in just the technological sense, I mean distributive justice, no more divisions between rich and poor. Everything seemed solvable. We'd only have to wait until other countries also understood it. We felt as if other people only had to read more books and then they'd also abolish everything that was wrong. Today it feels more like we can't understand anything and it can't get better at all. There seems to be no solution, only the destruction of structures and cultures.

TWR   *Visitation*, your third novel, centres on a house as a silent witness to history. You've written a lot about cities and places that seem to embody and reflect society, and places as a lieu de memoire.
JE   The older you get, the more stories you learn about the places you encounter, and your awareness is heightened precisely because you learn more. Things can suddenly get quite uncanny because you realise that things were there before you, and they will be there after you. That's when you begin to realise that you're just one chapter in a river of time. I have often thought about this: we know that time separates things from each other. And yet we also get the feeling that it could be fifty years ago, in the same room. You often have these visions that a room, a place, can focus history, can annul time in a strange way. I always thought it was fascinating to look at one and the same thing from different angles. Take for example a room, a house, a place. Ten people will tell you ten different stories about it.

I examined the question of home in *Visitation*. In every chapter the meaning is a different one. The architect tries to build the concept of home: how do you produce home technically, in a house? The Jewish girl: for her home is something that she no longer has. Her last home is herself. For the emigrants, home is something to do with language. In Germany, the relationship to the term 'home' is a difficult one – if you know what has been done with it. On the one hand you may say that people who speak German are those who live in your home. At the same time they may appear to you like total strangers because they thought in completely different ways from you. My grandparents, for example: they thought it was extremely uncanny what kind of people lived in their home country, and what they did, from a moral perspective.

When I walk through Berlin nowadays I constantly see two realities, the GDR reality and today's reality. It is extremely obvious here. Over there, that was a bomb crater and now there's a big fat house. Many places have been renamed, and you always keep it in mind, you don't just forget about it. In the countryside many streets are still named after famous anti-fascists. It is a relic of the past.

TWR   So places remember things?

JE   During the Nazi era buildings were designed to communicate a certain philosophy. The GDR had concepts that weren't dissimilar: they wanted to symbolise progress. Then, from one day to the next, the society that has produced these utopias is gone, but the buildings are still there. There's a real discrepancy here – but no one does anything. Everybody keeps using the buildings. Mahrzahn [a big GDR socialist housing project] evolved from the philosophy that everyone should be able to have a comfortable flat. Mahrzahn is now what it was meant to be when it was planned. The trees have grown tall. Everything that was ugly about it is now quite nice. The idea of humane living isn't so unbelievable anymore. Only the socialism that produced the concept has disappeared. Back then it was the goal for everyone to have light, friendly flats. If people get to live in them now, that's great. They just don't know why. There are unsolved remains there. I often think about that.

TWR   Is it fair to say that *Visitation* and *The End of Days* are twins? They seem to explore the same theme: to look at the German twentieth century through two different lenses, in *Visitation* through a house and in *The End of Days* through one person's life.

JE   That's probably just the same head and brain. I didn't see it that way, I wanted to write about two completely different things. In *Visitation* I wanted to write about a house. And then I wanted to write about death. The focus is different in each book. *The End of Days* follows its protagonist to many different places. These are mentioned in *Visitation*, but the house in Germany is always at the centre of the narrative – stories run through it and become visible exactly as they pass through. With *The End of Days* I wanted to explore the question what kind of coincidences make our life our life. There are different types of coincidence, banal ones and complex ones. That doesn't really happen in *Visitation*:

there we have real inevitability. When somebody has to go, they really have to go. It is about the immovability of circumstances.

TWR   What is your experience of your books being read in different languages and different countries?

JE   *Visitation* was translated into many different languages. I went to Indonesia, where students put on a ballet about the topic of home, inspired by the book. I did wonder: how did my book make it all the way to Indonesia? And then the stories began to appear, and it became apparent that of course people have to leave their houses in every country across the world, they have to flee everywhere.

Go Went Gone also touches on many topics that people know and can relate to: whether it's being confronted with bureaucracy, being rejected by a government department, or else the really central question of the book: how can I really know a person? Do I know them when I see their passport? Or do I only really know them when I... know them? When I know their real name? Or without their real name? Those are the kind of illusions that we in Europe like to indulge in: if we have a passport and a name, then we know who someone is.

I realised that people elsewhere think that the German policy regarding refugees was on the whole quite good, and that as a result they were surprised by *Go Went Gone*. It was interesting to see the reaction of American readers towards that book, because their experience of migration is completely different. They have learned from their experiences over the past two hundred years. Personally, however, I don't really believe that one can learn from history. I believe that every generation has to start from scratch. Of course we're influenced by our parents, our upbringing, but learning is tied to experience. It's connected to emotion, not just to books. The GDR is a good example. My grandparents' generation – communists – always stressed that we were lucky, that we were well off. We of course were bored to tears. Then the Wall fell and suddenly we realised that we needed 400 mark for rent. But where were we to get the money from? That's when we understood. You can't really hand experience down from one generation to another. One can say: a concentration camp is a terrible thing. One can go to a memorial, and if you're sensitive it will have an effect on you. But I have a friend whose aunt was in the gas chamber. She only just survived. That has a whole different kind of intensity. For others that is just a story, a sad story that is easily forgotten. But if that is my aunt, who comes over on Sundays to drink cups of coffee with me, then it's an entirely different thing.

TWR   Richard, the protagonist of *Go Went Gone*, has a unique approach to empathy...
JE   What I liked about Richard – or why I wanted to write him the way I did – was that he doesn't try to act as a good person. He is driven by an egotistical interest in understanding a major issue of his time, and he also has to deal with another problem, which is that he has to come to terms with himself. It is a simple question: what do you do when you're home all day, newly retired, and have nothing else to do? Society has rejected you, in a sense: your social circle, your routines are gone. None of us want to be reminded of the fact that we'll all die one day, and work is a great way to distract ourselves from it. But when you suddenly sit at home, by yourself, you're confronted with these questions. That is why he starts showing an interest in the group of refugees who are housed nearby: because he realises that they are in a similar position. They're being socially excluded, and they also have to come to terms with themselves. How are they dealing with it all? His interest isn't altruistic.

TWR   No, it's almost scientific.
JE   Yes, and I like that.

TWR   He's not exactly a do-gooder.
JE   No. I hope that I have avoided a certain type of vanity in that way, you know, 'He acts as a helper, he saves poor people' and so on. In some sense he has something of the naiveté that I described when I talked about children earlier, a kind of common sense that he uses to judge others by the same standards as he does himself and his kind. And that is what one should do, really. He has a naiveté, he hasn't yet learned about preconceived notions and differences between people. He's surprised at things. I felt the same way when I was doing my research. If I imagine that I was in his situation – and that is what I imagine all the time – then it all seems immensely difficult.

Two of the group that I talked to for my novel have just been rejected by the German asylum system for the last time. They have to go back to Italy. I always imagine what I would do in that situation. I think it's awful, every one of us would think it awful.

TWR   It is especially awful to consider the sheer randomness of who makes it and who doesn't. That people are being made dependent on luck, accident and strangers' sympathies.
JE   Yes, I often think about that too.

TWR   It does seem like people are only looking out for what they consider their own right now. It's a type of nationalism that is deeply rooted everywhere. Certainly that is the way that things feel in the UK at the moment.
JE   I wonder if we don't see racism appear in its purest form right now: if not even the otherwise all-powerful business community can hold its own against politicians [regarding refugees' and migrants' right to work]. We can only hope that all these people get comfortable in their elite status and die out soon. Many of the xenophobes in Germany aren't even aware how many rules and regulations there are to help German workers out.

TWR   Let's switch gears. What do you read?
JE   I read three different types of books: books for work, which I am of course interested in, but they're usually about something I'm researching. Then there are books by friends, and because I have more and more friends who write, that is a decent amount of reading. It is also interesting because one wants to know what other people are writing. And then there are books that I read for pure pleasure. And occasionally I win a prize and then I read the books of the person the prize is named after, for the acceptance speech.

TWR   When is a book well-written?
JE   Well. Let's put it this way, I know it right away, but I'm not a literary scholar – thank god! It's when someone is more concerned with the thing itself than with how they come across as an author. When they really want to understand something, when they write in order to understand. I think it's important that a writer is musical. You can feel despair about things, be deeply concerned about them, and still show a certain type of sovereignty in the sense that you have the power to exclude embellishments and flourishes, that you maintain a type of effortlessness, a sense of economy and sparseness.

To give you an example, I read Svetlana

Alexievich recently and she is incredible. That really is literature. The way she puts things together! There's resonance to it. I read *Second-Hand Time* last year. The connection she makes between the end of an empire and the racism between people who not so long ago were all part of the USSR, that is great. Something that opens up a lot of space for thought is good. What I thought was particularly great was that she interviewed people who said that they were first perpetrators and then victims. She leaves her readers alone with that open question. That is good literature. It is such a crazy idea, you can think about it for a long time and look at the world with that in mind, and you'll never be done thinking about it.

TWR   So good writing is having the courage to leave questions unanswered?
JE   Yes, and to recognise things as questions in the first place. Literature is not there to give ready-made answers, but to make dissonances audible. I am constantly being asked how we should solve the refugee crisis – as if I was Angela Merkel. Of course one could say that all of this is a waste of time, that we don't need art because we don't need more questions, we can see the questions by ourselves. But I'm thinking of questions that are also questions to ourselves – how are we going to deal with the fact that we see Auschwitz in the Mediterranean, how do we deal with the fact that we want to keep our prosperity at the expense of others?

TWR   So would you say that the task of literature is to remember things on behalf of society?
JE   I don't know if I'd say it's a task. But what literature can do is make things emotionally tangible, and it gives you the luxury of playing: you can try out what another life would look like. Empathy. What I try to do when I write is to look at things in a bigger context, both in terms of time and space, to put fears into a context with things that are bigger than one's own life. Or to look at how others in similar situations dealt with fear.
   Somehow, in some way, society produces writers, and it produces people who do other work. I'm not a plumber, I'm a writer. My father says that societies have a way of creating systems of order, and art has a specific function in this system. Sometimes I think that so many things are just a distraction: thinking about diets, cooking, bungee jumping – those seem to me like a strange kind of sideshow. But other people say that at least a small part of society has reached utopia, and everyone else may also reach it at some point.

TWR   What do you mean by utopia?
JE   Utopia means being able to do things just for pleasure. But I think that as long as there are people who drown in the Mediterranean and nobody cares, then that just isn't right. That may be unfair because the individual who is enjoying themselves is not at fault and not the cause. But as long as people are dying in horrible ways it just isn't okay. Of course there are also writers who say, Well that's the way it is, the elite is thriving and everyone else has to pay the price, and that's how it has always been. What I think is really problematic, though, is that we always think that we've reached the final conclusion over what is good and what is bad.

TWR   So you think that we don't know what's good and bad?
JE   You're always searching for it. But humanity has often thought that they know what's good and what's bad, and they were often completely different from what we think now. Of course I also think that I'm right about everything, but we always have to take into account that we're the products of our own time, the victims of our own history and education.

TWR   And as a writer what you produce is a result of that, of time, history and education.
JE   Yes. What I wish for is to be able to observe the stream of all of history. We have to keep searching for a way of living together that works better than what we have right now. Because what is happening right now is essentially war, and I don't like war. I believe that all parents love their children, and nobody wants their child to die in a war. A society where people stop considering other people's children as if they were their own: something has gone seriously wrong there. The only way we can escape that kind of egotism is to become part of a community. This desire is a basic need – the question is, who makes use of this basic need for their own purposes? Food isn't the only thing that people require. You have to think about all of these things in the abstract and in general, but you also have to master them in your own, personal life.

T. D.,
August 2018

VASHTI
ZAKIA UDDIN

FICTION

I met John at the dance summer school. He was standing at the lower set of doors towards the bottom of the hall, half-in, half-out, as if he was hoping to be missed. Cherri was sitting on the empty stage. The other girls had left half an hour ago. When she saw her father, Cherri picked up her yellow rucksack and walked towards us, her chunky pink trainers squeaking on the old lino. The building had once been a theatre and now served as a community centre. As she walked across the hall, I turned to him. Mr Smithley, I said, unable to finish my sentence. I wanted to say that he should have been there earlier. It did something to a child, always waiting for their parents. But he smiled, as though he had been expecting me, not the other way around. I fingered my pendant, readjusted my neckline. I could not tell what he wanted exactly: men were often baffled by my fantastical appearance in a banal environment.

He peered at the name badge pinned on my dress. Vashti, he said. Call me John. He held out his hand and, after a second, I had to withdraw mine because it started burning. So, he said, looking around me but not focusing on anything. What will my daughter learn in the next few months? Barbara's Premier Touring Dance School Makes Winners in the Essex Region, he read aloud from the promo poster tacked on the wall. Cherri waited, rubbing her itchy-looking ankles together. She looked nothing like John, with her red skin and fuzzy blonde hair. He frowned at her, like she was a fossil in a museum or something else that had once been interesting. The girls learn to dance and sing, I replied. And even if they don't go on to a career, they leave with our ethos to guide them through life. What's the *ethos*? he asked, baring small white teeth. Confidence, composure and commitment, I said. His confrontational manner implied great self-assurance or deep insecurity. I could not yet tell them apart.

Have you had a good time? he asked Cherri. I pretended to inspect my clipboard. Her bobbled ponytail bounced up and down in my peripheral vision. I'd noticed her straight away, with her white eczema gloves and thick glasses. She stood not so far from the other girls that it looked odd, but not so close that it was obvious they were ignoring her. During the breaks, she sat on the stage, looking at her flip phone. None of the other girls had phones. It gave her an air of privilege, along with her expensive professional dance clothes. But the clothes didn't quite fit, or match, in the same way that her skewed pigtails seemed to have been done absent-mindedly.

Before she could say anything, I put my hand on her shoulder. Cherri is a promising student, I said. I could feel her squinting up at me. John rubbed his neck, in the same way that she did. Well, I told you, he said. Didn't I say so? For a few seconds we were all connected, with his hand on her other shoulder, Cherri in the middle.

Over the following weeks, I introduced the girls to aspects of my spiritual practice. I drew them into a circle, made them link arms. Shut your eyes, I said. Visualising helps you achieve your innermost desires. I examined each face like a tarot card. There are no longer many respectable jobs where women get paid to dance *semi-adequately* – time runs out quickly! I said. Where do you want to be when you're eleven? Think, think! Sometimes a girl whispered, I just want my mum and dad to enjoy it. Is that all? I asked, trying not to look disappointed. Come up with better answers during break. I set the alarm clock on the empty stage, watched them clump into their corners. The hall began to smell of carbonated drinks and beefy crisps, which I had long come to associate with summer afternoons.

My interest in Cherri had grown, but she was suspicious of attention. She had not made any friends since the summer school had started. Even the shy, quiet pupils who were drawn to each other didn't speak to Cherri. Her self-styled outfits suggested neither parental devotion nor a compensatory burgeoning teenage sophistication. I was not one of those teachers who oversaw the classroom like an indifferent god. I had derived most of my teaching skills from a self-parenting book. When I looked at a troubled, lonely child, I assumed they had a hidden talent, that they were waiting to be called, just as dancing had called to me. I would like to see *you* dance, I said to Cherri, whenever she stood apart, shuffling her feet. I emphasised *you*. Once, she looked at me blankly. I *am* dancing, she had replied.

I had divided the girls into houses named after inspirational cultural icons. Cherri was in Britney House with Taylor, Manda and Emily, three girls who had been the town's carnival princesses in successive years. They wore matching dolphin charms which they liked to raise in the air and jangle at the same time. You should be in a different group, I heard Taylor telling Cherri and two other girls, twins with chunky glasses. She made circles around her eyes with her fingers. Taylor was ten, but looked thirteen. She wore belly tops and liked to beat her round, rubbery-looking stomach for her friends' amusement.

In the third week, each house performed a short sequence that they had devised themselves. Cherri ran on after Taylor and Manda, the pigtails she was too old for beating on either side. She moved like someone in the late stages of needing to pee, flexing her lower half urgently, bent over, her legs stiff as a column. She was unable to keep up with the others, so she had started improvising. The rest of the class were laughing. She carried on, without looking at them. When the twins ran on, Cherri slowed down, her limbs heavy, her face occupied.

I came up behind Cherri while the other girls were changing. Her back twitched but she didn't turn around. She was sitting on her own, already dressed, her rucksack next to her. It was tough today, wasn't it? I said. She didn't reply. I sat down. It took me years to get where I am. And I'm not even qualified yet! Would speaking to your father help? We could all get together, talk about your *confidence*. She shrugged. You could try. She said it in a disembodied way, like a ventriloquist's dummy, repeating it with an exaggerated slump of her shoulders.

I had often seen Mr Smithley – or John, as he said to call him – waiting in his car for Cherri. He had never looked across to see me staring. But calling would feel like we were carrying on a conversation, because he had been on my mind since I had first spoken to him, his smile with its even white incisors, and the way my hand burned. After class, I scrolled through the emergency contacts list on my phone. My heart beat faster. My nerves were unexpected. I had to swallow several times for fear that I would run out of air when he answered.

The ringing stopped. John, he said, as though he was going to be the subject of the conversation. It's Vashti, Cherri's teacher? Don't worry, nothing has happened. I feel we need to talk about Cherri's confidence. Obstinance, he said. Confidence, I repeated. Maybe her mum would want to come along. She died when Cherri was five. I'm so sorry. Is there anyone she might have for feminine guidance? I waited, cupping my mouth. Fiona, my wife. Of four years. But let's say there are many ways in which a marriage can be over. It's hard to be on your own, I said, before he had to explain further. You're very supportive, Vashti. Sometimes the most potentially able students are the least self-assured, I replied. He murmured yes, maybe we could talk about that over dinner. I laughed, because I didn't want him to think that I was naive. It would be deeply unprofessional of me, I said, thinking of how I had never been so compromised as to say those words before and how I might never be again.

The walls of Bonita's were mounted with muddy macros of flowers. Candles in dimpled red jars glowed on every table. The mid-tempo music was evocative of beaches and tropical weather, even though all I could see out of the big windows was the movement of the empty escalators. I was in Lakeside Thurrock, a giant shopping centre off the motorway. On the phone, John had said he liked its atmosphere – and that it was nice to get out of Wakesea for the evening. But he looked flustered when he came in, despite being early. The wet wrinkled half-moons of his underarms slid into view as he took off his unscuffed leather jacket. He sat down and looked around. I like to see what the big boys are doing, he said. Who are the big boys? I asked. The big boys of franchising. I'm in the franchising business, he said. Anyway, tell me about yourself.

The room went dark, light, dark as the candles flickered. I felt as though we were in a play and had to perform ourselves. Everything looked like a prop. I became nervous, the way I always did when anyone asked me to talk about my life. I had established facts about myself – I was once a dancer, now a modern jazz instructor for children. I was nearly twenty-seven. He slapped the table, so the cutlery jumped. I thought about being an actor when I was your age. He said *your age* dismissively, as if he had beaten me to my age in a race. I can do great impressions, he said. I don't watch television or the news, I said. You won't know who I'm impersonating then, he said, raising his eyebrows.

I might go back to dancing, I said. He examined the bowl of guacamole near my plate. You've been at the school a long time, he said. Have you heard of

YouTube? I asked him, my mind racing. I didn't know anything about YouTube, but it sounded impressive, like I was thinking big. We could film the girls dancing. Cultivate them as personalities. I just need to convince Barbara. The Tube, it's on the computer, isn't it? I'm not a computer guy, he said. Anyway, I can't really leave her, I said. She's given me a lot of opportunities. She built the dance school from the ground up. I recited what I had written on the funding application earlier that year: Barbara's is the most successful touring dance school in the eastern region.

I'm fascinated by *you*, he said. It was hard to explain to a self-made businessman that some of us got satisfaction from being needed in ways that didn't always confer authority. If everyone put themselves first, we'd be doomed. What do *you* want? he asked. It was the way he said *you*, as though I had never thought about myself before.

We stood in the car park facing each other. What's going on? I asked, because I had been telling myself not to ask. He moved forward, so I had to stare up at him. You intrigue me, he said. It seemed a strange thing to say after I had told him about myself. He wanted to pretend that he didn't know what was happening between us. I knew that meant we would see each other again. But the only way I could be sure of what he was thinking was to make him think the same as me. I grabbed his neck, drew him closer. He began kissing back after a few seconds. Hoo, he said afterwards, I wasn't expecting that. He looked at me sideways. It reminded me of how I had been told to look at goats in the petting zoo when I was younger, but I think he was trying to show me that he was shy or that it was his best angle.

Barbara seemed to know that something had changed. She called me to her office for a catch-up session. While I had never purposely kept anything from Barbara, I thought it best not to tell her about John. It was nice not to share something with my boss, as though I had a lurid piece of gossip about myself. He had called me the previous night. He spoke on the phone with a different voice and I pretended not to know him as he told me his sexual fantasies.

During summer, Barbara and I relocated the school to various coastal towns in Essex. The rest of the year, we had a small studio in Colchester. Barbara drove back every night, and because I still hadn't learnt to drive, I rented a place in whatever town we were staying in and sublet the little flat I had in Colchester. But her office felt the same wherever we went. The scent of clary sage which she pumped into the air every few hours to relieve her tension. The blinds always down.

Have you heard of YouTube, Barbara? Par-don, she said, adjusting her glasses and then the golden orb she wore around her neck. Whenever I suggested anything new to do with the business, she became tired or her hearing went, so that it was embarrassing to repeat myself. Nothing, I replied. I've seen you moping, Vee. I'm not going to be around forever, she said, again. The first time, I'd thought she had cancer or some other terminal illness, but she had been saying it for a year now.

You have to *empower* yourself. She reached for the clary sage. Long walks, flower-arranging, learning Italian, weight-lifting, decoupage, kick-boxing – pick one, she said, when I asked her how. Empowerment sounded lonely. She was trying to hand me my freedom in the way that people do – teasingly, haltingly. But I was afraid, so I said I was happy.

John and I went to another restaurant in the shopping centre. I called our dates parents' evenings and he thought it was because of his age, not because he was a parent. At the restaurant, he made notes, asking me to rate it on a five-point scale for service, presentation and ambience. I kept thinking of what Barbara had said, about empowering myself. Pasta kept falling out of my mouth, like I couldn't concentrate on doing two things at once: eating and looking normal. What's wrong? he asked. We both watched my unchewed gnocchi land back onto the plate. My jaw snapped the empty air. Work, I said. Afterwards, we drove back to Wakesea, the water flat and black below us, the town's outline sawtoothing the sky.

White lozenges of motorway signs dissolved into the dark and we were finally in the town, winding past the tiny houses. He put the radio on, a song that had been playing from every car and shop all summer. The chorus went *carry on having fun, fun, fun / never stop being young.* This is such an odd place for a lone woman to move to, he said. He said 'lone woman' in a quavering voice like someone might say 'lone killer'. I've always wanted to move around for my work, I said. But it probably wouldn't have happened if Barbara hadn't called the day after the psychic. I stopped speaking, changed the radio station. What psychic? He glanced at me, and then looked away swiftly, as if he was worried I would answer. I shook my head. Nothing. My road came into view. It was always quiet, as though the other residents had fled.

I lived in a rented house at the end of the terrace. John peered out at its lit windows. He didn't turn the engine off. Why are the lights on? I do it to put off the burglars, I replied. I've told you that. He had never come into my house before. I asked him nervously whether he was going to get out. He leaned over and kissed me, mouth pursed. And then he moved back and stared ahead, seemingly waiting for me to leave. Well, I'll hear from you soon, I said. I got out and slammed the door. The night air was cold coming in from the sea. It tapped my chest and my bare arms. I searched for my key, hoping it wouldn't take so long that it looked like I was waiting for him, but also that I wouldn't find it so quickly that I would disappear into the house and he would forget about me, about us.

The car idled outside as I stood in the hallway and stared into the mirror. My make-up had run. I looked like a child's drawing of a dangerous stranger.

Lipstick bleed, mascara pitted around my eyes. Was that why he hadn't come in? No one withheld for that long. When I went into the kitchen, the floor was covered in slugs. They must have come in when it rained. But it was now so hot again that they had dried up. I didn't have any cutlery, or anything sharp, apart from a nail file that I had left on the counter. I knelt down on the floor and scraped up one greying slug with the file and threw it into the bin. Then I walked back into the living room to draw the curtains. The halogen bulb made the fat pink roses on them swim. I switched it off and lifted a curtain. John was watching me from the car, his face grainy in the darkness. I imagined him as a strange man compelled by my every move. I walked to the door slowly and waited for him to knock.

At the end of each class, the girls practised their routine for the show. There were two weeks left before the finale. The better dancers had solos, the less good ones were part of the general chorus. Cherri danced by herself in a corner of the room. She had not come to resemble John, but sometimes I could see him crouched behind her eyes, watching me. It made me want to reach an uncomplicated part of him. Cherri, shouldn't you be over there? I pointed to the other back-row dancers who were watching us. I realised that the abrupt movements that she was making were part of a sequence that she had devised herself.

You said that you wanted to see me dance, she said. Cherri had not yet learnt how to synchronise her arms and legs. She could still only move one set of limbs at a time. My self-parenting guide had taught me that handling such moments wrongly could be permanently damaging, that my words could one day pound in her head like blood. You have to practise a lot to do a solo, I said. People have expectations, not just me but all the people who will watch you. I know, she said, as if that was unimportant. We could dance together after class. Just you and me, I said.

She peered down at her new-looking trainers. The soles lit up and were inappropriate for dancing. I can do it myself, she said. But you can help if you want. Will your dad come to the finale? I asked, after a few seconds, as if it was an afterthought. She nodded. We could work on a dance that will impress him, I said. She looked up sharply. I don't want to impress him, she said, I just don't want to be in the back row.

Have you been with an older man before me? John asked a few days later. I said yes. He looked disappointed. I picked up the oil bottle from the side of the bed and put it into the cupboard, which was mostly empty, apart from a few toys I had bought in anticipation of tonight. He lay on the bedsheets, his head behind his hands, his body stiff, like he was imitating someone relaxing. This house is so unlived in, he said. What's your house like? He didn't answer. Will you put pictures up if you stay? he asked. He kept looking around at the bare walls. No, I don't think so, I said. I hadn't noticed before that they had nothing on them.

I lay down next to him and put my head on his chest. Staring up at the ceiling, I noticed for the first time that someone had traced a smiley face with the gloss paint. Terrible things happened to you once, he said. Before we met, he added. I didn't know how he knew, but it made me think that we could connect. When people shared their most terrible and life-changing experiences, they were more likely to fall in love. It wasn't just a coincidence Barbara found me when she did, I said.

I thought about it every day but when I told it, gaps inserted themselves. The order became confused. I left home and moved to a bedsit in London where I spent every night circling job adverts in *Loot*. I stopped dancing because classes were too expensive. Something had to change but I didn't know who could change it, I told John. And then a business card came through the letterbox. It was from a real psychic called Nebula. I called and made an appointment. I went to Nebula's place in Camden. She stood in the hallway, vest top sliding down her shoulders, cargo pants falling off her skinny hips. She led me through some beaded curtains that kept on swinging and knocking against each other as we walked down another corridor. There were laminated pictures of ethereal, pastel women on the walls. She took me into a small, dark room with a white plastic table and two chairs, which looked like garden furniture.

Nebula sat me down, drew my arms into the centre. She closed her eyes, squeezed my fingers. We held hands until the table started shaking and she began digging her nails into my skin. The whites of her eyes became so big it was like they'd been boiled. You're cursed, she said. I need £50 to lift the curse. That was the exact amount that I had saved from my dole for next month's rent. I don't have £50, I said. She sighed, got up and switched the light on. Started opening one cupboard after the other, leaving them ajar. We were in a kitchen but there was no food anywhere or anything that might be useful: no plates, no cups, just a polystyrene container with dried noodles hanging from its lip. When she turned to me, she had an armful of green candles. She bundled them towards me: Take these, burn as many as you can, she said.

I went back to my bedsit with the candles in a carrier bag. I drank three cups of lumpy instant coffee and lit each candle, watching until they burnt to nubs. I fell asleep before the last one. The next morning Barbara called me on my phone and said that she had a job for me. I had applied for so many that I didn't know who she was or what she was talking about, but I said I'd take it.

I didn't tell John about the fire. When I stopped talking, he was sitting upright, staring at the door. It was past midnight. You should speak to some-one, he said. About what? I asked. The curse, he said. By someone, he meant a professional. Not him. After a few minutes, he got up and started looking for his trousers. I need eight hours of sleep every night, he said. I always need eight hours, whatever happens. He laid out his trousers on the bed before going to the bathroom, clutching his white pants in his fist. His peeing was loud, as if he were pouring water out of a bucket into the toilet. It went on for ages. He came back into the room and sat down next to me. His underwear sagged below his rounded stomach. I wanted to reach out and stroke the soft hairs tufting in the dough. There's no such thing as a psychic, he said. Just charlatans. I know, I replied. I wondered what it would be like to be Cherri, and whether he patted her head in the same way.

John stopped calling and pretending to be a stranger. He said that he wanted to see me in person only, me as me. In the meantime, Barbara was away and I was in charge of the school. I had never been in charge, not in seven years of assisting her. I paid the rent on the hall, I checked in with parents, I updated our website. My anxieties were being stealthily replaced by new ones, like when people's homes get made over on weeknight television by well-meaning friends and neighbours. What if I stayed in one place? What if I pursued my own dream of dancing in front of adults?

There was a week left before the finale. I went to the little room at the back of the building where I liked to get ready after class. It had been a dressing room when the building was a theatre. Everything was stripped out except for a small table and a mirror with lightbulbs around it, the kind you imagine an actress would use in a melodrama. There were framed posters on the wall for amateur performances of *Grease* and *West Side Story*. Boxes of abandoned props stacked against the walls. I felt the emptiness of the whole place behind the door, as though I might step out into nothing. I started taking my day make-up off; putting my night make-up on. I was seeing John that evening. There was a knock, as I began swiping my cheeks.

I had watched the last girl leaving, waited for the clang of the front entrance shutting behind her. There should have been no one left. Cherri's snot-bubble voice came through the door: are you there? Can I come in? I thought you'd gone, I said. I opened the door. She stood, coat draped over one arm, milky thumbprints on her glasses. Dad says he's going to be late, she said. She wriggled onto a patchy velvet stool in the corner. We had not been alone together for any length of time since the first day of the summer school.

In the mirror, I watched her twist around and look at the boxes. Are you getting dressed for something? You look so beautiful, she said, digging her fingers below her gloves. I like to be ready for anything, I replied. I didn't want her to think that she had to wear make-up to look beautiful. But it was important to be prepared. Beauty on the inside is fine and everything, but it's not going to last forever, I said. The world can make you feel terrible about yourself. I glued on my lashes. Can I ask you questions? she said. I made a noise that could not have been construed as either yes or no, in an attempt to politely deter her. I had been careful not to pay too much obvious attention to Cherri, but I had not thought that she was paying attention to me.

Do you have secret children, Vashti? Where would I keep them? I said. I believe that it's immoral to do anything but adopt. She opened her mouth, and kept it open, staring blankly at me. When I started to explain, she laughed. The game was to say things that shocked her. Vashti, do you have a secret husband? Because you're old. Not old like Fiona. Or like my mum was. But *oldish*. My lash glue was starting to drip onto my cheeks. There were no windows in the room, no air. I pulled the lashes off. It's the twenty-first century and you will no longer learn anything meaningful by asking women these questions, I said. If you really want to know someone, in a deep and substantial way, you ask them things like – do you make your bed every day? Do you read your horoscopes every day? Do you *believe* in them? I paused for breath. Did you practise psychokinesis as a child? My voice started to shake. Write those down, I told her.

I don't know what psychokeenis is, she said. Psycho-kee-nee-ses, I said. It's the power of moving things with your mind. That's not real, she said. Is your father on his way? I asked. The glue was webbing my fingers together, I was starting to feel hot. The phone buzzed before I could get up. She shouted: He's here! and threw up a little fist in the air.

I'll come with you, I said. I'm old enough to go on my own, she said. You don't know who's out there, I said. I hiked up my mesh tights, arched into my heels. Cherri rolled her gloves back up. We left the dressing room. She put her hand in mine. Outside, the air was shimmering, the horizon smeary like a dirty window. In the distance, I could see John leaning against his car. His hair was pouffed out and he wasn't wearing his leather jacket, just a suit jacket like most businessmen his age.

John looked up as I smiled at him. He grimaced but maybe he was just tired from franchishing all day. He waved weakly, glanced at Cherri before getting back into the driver's seat. There's your dad, I said. She scanned the road, finally noticing the car. How did you know which one it is? I just guessed, I replied. Aren't you going to say hello? she asked. I should return to the school, I said, knowing that it would be wrong to go any further.

John called me that night, after our date. When the phone rang, I thought it was coming from outside of the house. My mobile never rang unexpectedly. The dialling code was for a landline. John had always rung from his mobile, sometimes withholding his number to make it suspenseful. But I knew it was him each time because I only heard from him in the middle of the night. I can't keep doing this, he said, when I picked up. I stared at the smiley face on the ceiling. I tried to focus, remembering the advice in the self-parenting book about grounding panicked children. I hadn't yet asked him any questions when he started speaking again. You have expectations of me that you're unwilling to admit, he said. What if I did, I said, even though I hadn't expected him to fulfil any. I can't fulfil them, he said, as if reading my mind. I had *low* expectations, I clarified. That's passive-aggressive, Jackie, he said. Who's Jackie? I asked. He coughed loudly, cutting off my question. Stop contacting me, he said. His throat caught, so I had to bring the phone right up to my burning ear to hear him. It was a mistake and you took advantage of my vulnerability. Before I could reply, I heard a woman's voice whisper loudly in the background: put the phone down, John. You've told her now.

I didn't switch my mobile off for the rest of the night. Its red death signal started blinking in my peripheral vision. That was not the end of it. I would not allow someone to be so cowardly. I grabbed the bed sheet which had been crumpled in the corner since John's last visit. He had slapped vanilla oil on my body and made minute adjustments to it as we had sex. My limbs had been cold, oil had stained the Egyptian cotton. I dragged the sheet to the kitchen like a dirty wedding train and stuffed it in the washing machine. A greasy trail glittered in the semi-darkness. On the counter were some half-empty beer cans from when John had last been around. I opened the back door. It had rained; the smell of meaty wet earth dizzied me. I emptied the rain out of the bowl I kept on the step and poured in the dregs to stop the slugs coming in, but it was too late.

Barbara called me in for a meeting when she came back. The blinds in her office were down again, the lamps were on, the room smelled of clary sage. I was trapped in her sunglasses like a slow-moving target. She said that she had good news for me: she wasn't ready to retire yet. It wasn't for her, slowly losing all her functions like an outmoded piece of technology. I'm going to look into YouTube, though I'm unconvinced. It'll never catch on. She sniffed, took a deep breath. But the good news is that I want you to take over the day-to-day running of the school.

She leaned forward so we were only a few inches apart. I could see reflections of myself everywhere: her glasses, the golden orb that she had around her neck. If you want to, of course, she said. I knew she was waiting for my answer. I didn't tell her that I had imagined myself somewhere else next year. The image – a big city nowhere near a sea, a waiting audience – wouldn't disappear. I hadn't even visualised it. It was as instantly familiar as an advert. She moved back, put her fingers on the orb and made me disappear. Don't be afraid of change, she said. There's only so many fires that one person can accidentally start.

John texted me before the class that day: *I wd like to c u. Things bad. But that not why. Come to beach cafe with C*. He always used text speak, even though I replied in full sentences. I wanted to weep. Something was pressing against the inside of my chest, a balloon swollen with water. I walked around the hall, watching the girls as they rehearsed for the finale. They were singing the song they had chosen for the dance: *fun fun fun fun*. A spitty croon through a girl's new teeth – was anything as sweet? It was the last time that I would see them dancing before the show. Time goes quickly! I said. Practise! In the corner, I could see Cherri dancing as if someone invisible was trying to push her over. She was practising her solo, the one that I said I'd help her with.

I remembered the bits about consistency in the self-parenting book, how important it was to treat the child of a man who had humiliated me like any other. Be the most consistent person in your life, the book said. Can I copy you? I asked Cherri. If I learn your dance, you can see how it looks. And then you can change it if it's not working. She nodded. I began moving, imitating her steps, fluidly bringing them together. That's not right, she said, staring at my feet. You're making it *different*. I stopped. She looked embarrassed, as if I were the one who couldn't dance.

Can I ask you a question? No one was nearby. Do you know anyone called Jackie? Or maybe Jacqueline? Cherri's pigtails flapped as she slowed down. How do you know about Jackie? she replied. I don't know her. Who is she? I asked. Cherri wobbled on one foot, shielded her face. I gestured for her to put her arms down. Her face was redder than usual. Jackie was a bird who used to sit outside my window, she said. Not a real one – well, she was *sort of* – she was my 'imaginary friend'. Cherri did quote marks in the air. She had big purple feathers and would make loud noises in the middle of the night. She couldn't fly, like a dodo or an ostrich can't fly, she said. Cherri carried on speaking but I couldn't hear her anymore. Was I a private joke between them, the father and daughter unit? I wanted to vomit, but I pinched my neck instead to retain my composure.

Later, I saw Taylor approaching Cherri. I watched them from the back of the class. Cherri looked at Taylor suspiciously. They had not spoken to each other – as far as I had seen – since I first placed them in Britney House together. Taylor rarely spoke to anyone but her friends. She liked to jangle in unison at the other girls. She liked to intimidate them with her height and comedy stomach beating. I could always intervene if anything happened between them. Or I could just watch. Who was I to think that Cherri needed my help in every situation?

I began circling. I stopped near them, looked into the middle distance. If you point your toes when you do the step, it's easier, I heard Taylor saying. Do this – she started spinning – and keep it pointed. She danced out Cherri's steps, her eyes trained on Cherri to make sure she was watching. When she stopped, Cherri copied her, moving faster with confidence. She finished more quickly than she expected, looking surprised when she neatly rounded off the sequence. Taylor beat her stomach: You can do it! she said. Cherri stared, before beating back: Yes, I can!

I reread John's text as Cherri and I left for the beach. I can't believe you're coming too! she kept saying, as we walked down the deserted road. I thought of Jackie the bird, flapping hopelessly at the window. The flat glaze of oil on the bed sheet. John was sitting outside the only cafe on the stretch that led to the pier, where all the daytrippers and carers gathered. His suit was rumpled and he was spooning ice cream from a bowl. He hadn't noticed us coming. We had never seen each other in stark daylight.

He nodded at me, before turning to Cherri, who was now standing at the table looking at the dessert. He took a five pound note out of his wallet and handed it to her. Take this, he said. Get what you want. Apart from the ice-cream. He stuck his arms out, puffed his cheeks and moved from side to side like an inflatable mascot in a storm. If you want to eat something fatty you have to pay for it yourself, Cherri said in a robotic voice. Exactly, he said. She grabbed the five pounds and went into the cafe, stamping her feet on the concrete.

After the door closed behind her, John turned to me, focused on the empty bowl. I'm sorry about the Jackie thing, he said. Why did you call me Jackie? I asked. Fiona found the extra phone, she made me call her – you, he said. I couldn't tell her it was Cherri's teacher. Not a one-off. As for Jackie – I can't remember where the name came from. He looked down, fiddled with the spoon. My feelings had been hurt, I told myself. And then she left, he said. She cut her hair a few weeks before. It was like this. He made a box-like shape around his head. Very neat, very sensible, he said sadly. She made me call you and she bloody left anyway. And took the car. I had to walk all the way down here. His shoulders fell, dried sweat flaked off his forehead.

Cherri came out of the cafe, carrying a can of Fanta. I'm going to the beach, she said. She dropped the change on the table. We watched her cross the empty road and disappear down the steps. No one came to that stretch of the beach: it was too far from the pier, and most people in Wakesea were old or had mobility problems. We could see Cherri walking near the groynes, stopping to look across at us, small as we were. She'll be fine, he said. We used to come to this beach a lot when she was little, with her mum. He looked up at the sky, as if she were hovering above us.

I know you're disgusted, he said, after a few seconds of respectful silence. You hate me, don't you? I don't *hate* you, I began. You *should* hate me, he said. Are you going to stay? he asked, after I didn't reply. As in, are you going to stay after the school ends? I thought of Barbara, of all the coastal towns ahead, of an audience waiting in a darkened room. Without wanting to, I caught his eyes brightening, even though he didn't know what I was undecided about.

Tinny, familiar music rose from the beach. It was the finale song: *never stop being young/fun fun fun*! In its pauses, we heard a phlegmy cough turning into laughter. We both looked towards the sea, the sand. There was no one there, no sign of Cherri. John got up, brushed down his ill-fitting suit. I followed him across the road, stopped with him at the ramp that led to the beach. Below, there was no sign of recent occupation, apart from a jagged red bucket that was half-buried in pebbles. Cherri, he shouted over the music. The ramp was covered in a lurid green slime. He turned to look for another way down. The laughter broke out again. We both leant over the iron railing. In a recess only visible when we craned forward was a balding man sitting on a crate. Lined neatly next to him was a portable radio, a thin blue carrier bag and a pair of old brown shoes. He was rocking back and forth with laughter. If his hands hadn't been wrapped around his knees, he would have fallen headfirst into the sand. In front of him was a small pink cowboy hat I recognised from the school's prop box. Cherri came out from the recess, wearing her finale costume, her other dress sticking out from underneath it, so she looked twice her normal size.

The man began to clap. She started dancing, hesitating between each step. John reached over the railings, yelled her name. The music was too loud. He stuck a foot onto the mossy ramp. He would have to go further down to the other set of steps in order to get Cherri, or risk sliding down the slope and injuring himself. He would have to leave her there with the man, just for a minute or two. He couldn't decide. I shouted her name. She went on dancing, grimacing and mouthing numbers to herself. It was the first time I had seen her whole solo, its steps in sequence. She moved without pause. She twirled, both of her dresses flying up and exposing her red thighs.

She stopped and punched her gloved arms in the air, one after the other. Jumping back, she stumbled and recovered with a big smile. She was sure of herself. I had never known her to be so confident, so composed. The old man threw some coins into the hat, they glinted in the sun. Cherri, what are you doing? John shouted as the finale song segued into a tune I hadn't heard before. Cherri looked around and up. The old man was walking past her quickly, carrier bag dangling from his wrist, shoes held to his chest. She saw her father, waved. He didn't wave back, just stood there, his hand on his chest, breathing heavily. Her gaze went from him to me, and back again. She ran to the hat, picked it up carefully, stared back up at us. Look! she shouted. Can you see me? I'm here! I'm here!

RENATE BERTLMANN

Austrian artist Renate Bertlmann began developing a language for female erotics in the 1970s. Her photographs, sculpture, performance, and film do not shy away from obscenity, sadism or sexual fetish. Latex teats squeak against one another, wrinkled condoms hang from washing lines, nipples become razors. Deflated sex dolls lie, post-fuck, on bedroom floors.

In the ten-part sculpture 'Urvagina' (1978), long tendrils of latex spill from slits in a row of white boxes. Bertlmann interacted with the objects she made, treating them as bawdy props. One photograph shows her holding a box between her open legs. The latex curls around her feet, like strings of pearls or seaweed: a representation of female ejaculation. 'Urvagina' is also a joke on the idea of an essential, original gender, a theme to which Bertlmann has returned. In the series 'René ou Reneé' (1976–7), she photographs herself in different guises: dressed in a suit as an office worker, her hands clasped around an imaginary dick; in a top hat with her tongue out; baring her teeth at a velvet-covered table. Gesturing towards the surrealist porn of René Magritte, the images in 'René ou Reneé' are intended to be provocatively slapstick. Is this René or Reneé, she asks? Man or woman?

When Bertlmann's work was first shown she came in for heavy criticism, from radical feminists and conservatives alike. Visitors to the exhibition *Museum des Geldesat* at the Städtische Kunsthalle Mannheim in Düsseldorf in 1978 called for her photographs and sculptures – including a shrine for a penis, inscribed 'San Erectus' – to be removed, and for the artist to be prosecuted. When the show toured, both Centre Pompidou and Van Abbemuseum refused to include her. Anti-porn feminists in the 1980s also took umbrage at her use of sexual imagery, and labelled her 'phallus-addicted'.

In recent years attitudes towards Bertlmann have changed, and her work has been embraced by the institutional sector. In 2014 she participated in the Gwangjui Biennale, and her work has been exhibited at Tate Modern (2015), MUSAC, Leon (2015) and Hayward Gallery (2018).

PLATES

I

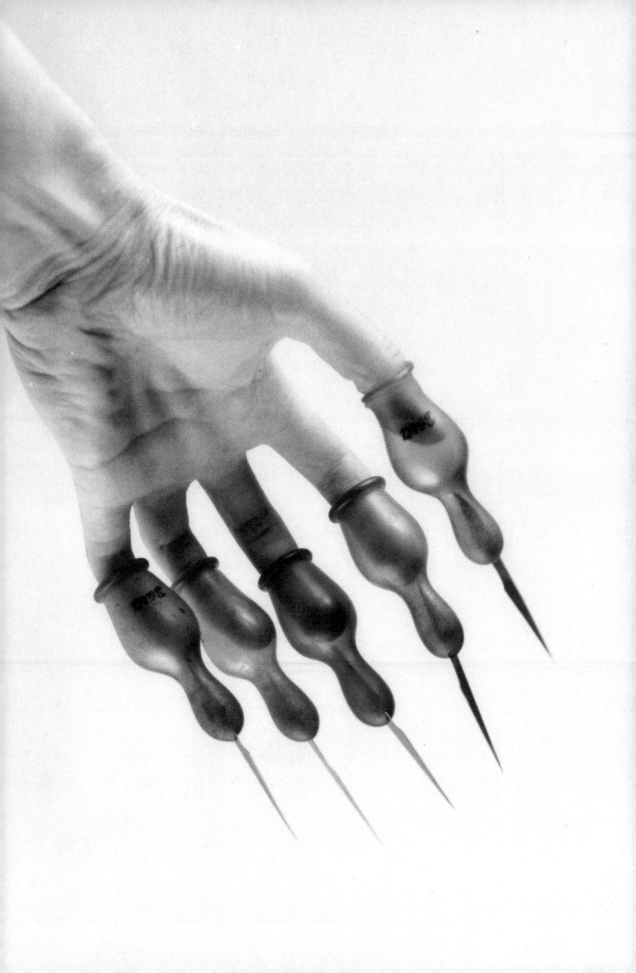

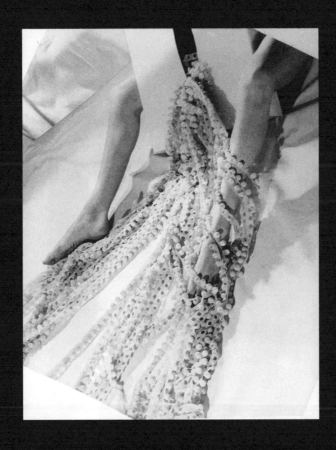

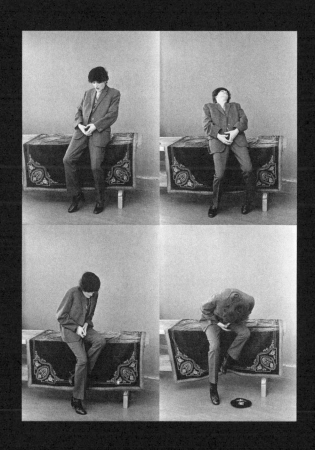

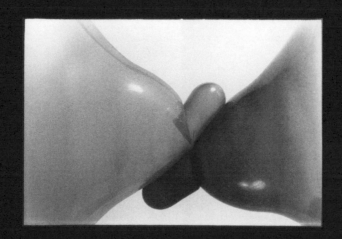

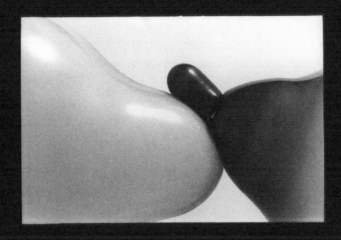

New York,
My love –
I hope that I did not
hurt you by revealing to
you all my dreams and
fears. Only

New York. 18/1/80

My Love –
I hope that I did not
hurt you by revealing to
you all my dreams and
fears. Only one thing I am
longing for: to touch your
body with my body and to
touch your Soul with mine.
Please do answer me
yours for ever
Renate

HEATHER CHRISTLE

OUR TOWN

We can tell that he's the mayor
because of his long hat.
The mayor always wears
a long hat says the historical society
which annually celebrates
the founding of itself.
It's not a bad job
being mayor says the mayor
in his inaugural address.
I get so mad when people
address me. I feel like red foam.
So I am roaring around in the interior
and thinking about writing
something nasty on the wall.
But the mayor is not a bad guy.
I was there when he found his long hat
soon after developing
the faculty of speech.
Meanwhile, playing around
with my little toe, it broke right off.
Leave it alone, they always said.
Well now I'll have to.

A CRIMINAL

They put a cabbage on trial
The judge said what are the charges
They didn't have any

Charges cost $7 each
They only had $4
and that was for milk etc.

They let the cabbage go
It rolled around
Rolled down to the judge's house

The judge's children looked out the window
saw the cabbage
They weren't afraid

They adopted the cabbage
Gave it a name
Now it sleeps

in a shoebox full of feathers
yanked from the corpse
of my goose

ANY DISTANCE MAY BE CALLED A REMOVE

I have no sense of proportion

I was born without one

Where my sense of proportion should have been a nurse found instead a small doily

Small is the word she used

In my mind it is delicate and blue, as are certain mountains

How calming is a mountain in these uncertain times

At the end of a run I squatted to watch ants swarm from a crack in the sidewalk

I could not discern the cause

A woman came out of her house and swarmed over to me

Are you alright she asked

I could not construct a true reply

In the picture of the view from her window I was what's wrong

And the ants gave me joy

How much I cannot say

NETFLIX

The sky likes to pretend it is watching a documentary series about itself

Every day representing the kind of quiet shot that will show what it is really like

Pink morning, stratus afternoon, not the night

The night is the sky's older sister and not the subject of this documentary series

The sky can't decide on the right narrator or font for captions

In distress the sky thinks it will have a very low-key and understated style

It will have nothing but intricate colour and occasional hawks

This is why no one will ever make this documentary explains God in the elevator at Netflix

The sky is a boring megalomaniac

God is on his way to pitch a show about elbows

They are probably going to say no

WHOLE CLOTH

I was wandering the earth in search of a mystical experience

I got my hopes up with a system of pulleys and buckets

I think pulleys must have been named by a baby

I mean come on

In the department store I became confused about the difference between
  mysticism and perfume

I smelled expensive like an expensive man

It seemed important to locate a mountain

I closed my eyes and tried to sense when the land sloped up

I became confused about the difference between altitude and aptitude

I wandered closer to the road

When people seem terrible I try to remember that once they were babies

Babies are terrible drivers

They cannot control their limbs or their emotions

Once I reached the mountain's apex I became one again

God swaddled me in a cloud

Though I struggled I could not get out

COMMON PRAYER

I have received the instructional kit

It contains everything I need

The reflective vest fits comfortably and reflects an adequate amount of light

The words go *Would that I were other than I am*

And there is a URL for problems

But I remain and the vest remains

And the incense is still pluming nicely around my unchanged form

I go to the website and I am the only one online

One time I heard God kept an AOL email address as a little joke

I heard God has always wanted to try windsurfing

I heard when you die the ellipses disappear and you finally get to see what
      God's been typing this whole time

The instructional kit mentions none of this

There is beautiful packaging piled up all around me

I try unzipping the vest halfway

It comes with free shipping and free returns

ON TRANSLATION ROUNDTABLE

In May 2017, during the tense weeks leading up to the opening of negotiations on the terms of Britain's withdrawal from the EU, the European Commission president Jean-Claude Juncker delivered a speech in Florence which drew applause from his audience, and scorn from British right-wing media. Halfway through his speech, he switched language. 'I'm hesitating between English and French,' he said, 'But I've made my choice. I will express myself in French because slowly but surely English is losing importance in Europe.'

The move was mostly gestural – calculated, and delivered with a glint in his eye – but revealing nonetheless: our split from Europe would begin first through language. The EU had once been happy to extend itself towards us, and to translate its edicts into our language. Now, we would need to do the translating; the burden to understand and to be understood would be ours. But why had we ever assumed it should be any other way?

In contemplating Brexit, and its questions of language, identity, nationalism, cooperation and compassion, we found we were in fact contemplating the issues of translation. Our roundtable is a chance to grapple with these ideas and to explore how language, and by extension translation, has the power both to let in and keep out. Or, as Khairani Barokka describes it, to be 'absence, sanctuary and weapon'.

During the course of the roundtable, participants talked about Brexit, colonialism and xenophobia, representation and accessibility, vulnerability and empathy. Alongside a consideration of the work of professional translators, they discussed the often unrecognised (care) work of interpretation that happens in immigrant communities every day. They noted the importance of oral cultures and multilingual texts, and the liberating power of not translating a text. They recognised that we all live in translation.

In her book-length essay on translation, *This Little Art*, Kate Briggs describes a somewhat similar language 'switch' to Juncker's. In Helen Lowe-Porter's English translation of Thomas Mann's *The Magic Mountain*, two characters suddenly start speaking French to one another, drawing the reader's attention to the artifice of their reading experience. 'I come up against the belief I suspended,' writes Briggs. 'So this was *never* in English, then. This was *always* in German.'

As Briggs argues in her book, translation challenges our beliefs as readers, and as citizens. If the following discussion reveals anything it's that translation allows us to hold two, or more, conflicting ideas in our minds at any one time; it reminds us that no language or literature belongs purely to one country; it models collaboration over individualism; and shows how uncertainty is as important to art-making as certainty. After all, why should we have to make a choice, like Juncker? Hesitating between one language and another can be the most exciting place to start from.

ŽELJKA MAROŠEVIĆ   Issue 24 of *The White Review* will be published around the time of Britain's withdrawal from the EU, as it stands. As we contemplate that moment and the nationalism that led to Brexit, I want to start by asking: is translation into English always a good thing? What are the dangers of making a text English, so to speak?

RAHUL BERY   There was a *Guardian* Longread article recently that basically presented English as a virus. And I kind of agree with that. I'm almost dismayed at how much people speak English. There's a bit in *Flights* by Olga Tokarczuk where the narrator is talking about being in airports and she says how she feels sorry for English people because they don't have a private language. Everyone can understand them. And it's like, what about us poor native English speakers, if you don't have any other choice but to speak in English? You know, English may be the language of commerce in airports but it's also my private language. It's the only way I can express myself.

And you're right, we always talk about translating literature into English as if it's this wonderful, novel thing, but that also implies that no one can read in any other language. I'm often dismayed at the spread of English rather than happy about it. I know there's a kind of utopian element to it as well. Maybe I should be happy that the Tower of Babel thing is finally wearing off the human race. But I don't really see it like that.

'FLUENCY IS POWER'

KATE BRIGGS   I work in an international art school in Rotterdam where the teaching language is English. The students come from all over Europe, some from outside of Europe, and we all work in English. Some of my colleagues are working in their second language – they're German, Serbian or Dutch.

I think it's really important to make it into a question. Because I think the problem is when it goes without saying that, of course this is what we're doing because this is our pragmatic language of sharing and communication. The problem is when it's not even raised as a potential issue, or something to think about and deal with, especially when I'm asking the students to write in English as their second or even third language.

Fluency is power, isn't it? The fluency of having an easy, unquestioned relationship with a language that is the dominant language, is a power,

is a privilege. So an awareness of those dynamics are really important. I know for myself, when I'm trying to express myself and be articulate in French, it's different to what I'm doing right now. And so that demand we make of the non-native English speakers is a demand. And it should be something that we are constantly thinking about and aware of.

But I know the question was about translating. An argument I've heard made which I think is true, is that it's because bilingualism is so much more of a rarity in the UK, compared to say in the Netherlands, that we are so celebratory and excited, or overexcited, by receiving translations into English. So this idea of: let's actually generate new prizes for translation, that's specific to an English-speaking culture.

ISOLATIONISM; IMPERIALISM

JAKOB STOUGAARD-NIELSEN   In many other places translation is seen as a norm, it's not something you're particularly concerned with, it's not a genre you choose your literature from. And it gets more attention. I agree with your point, Kate, that a multilingual society is probably more prone to receiving literature in translation and they are probably more open to the possibility of reading literatures from other countries. And why, for instance, should Romanian everyday life stories not be as interesting to people here as stories from Kansas in the US? There's something not quite right in terms of what we choose to pay attention to.

And we do see this leading, I think, to the kind of isolationism that Brexit is an expression of. This sense that we don't get anything of value from other language areas in Europe. I think that is underpinning it. So on the one hand, I think it's important to say that the diminishing multilingualism in English school systems, in the general populace, over the past twenty years has had a huge impact on the way that we understand translated literature. However, strangely enough, there are more books than ever published in translation in the UK. I mean, we hear about the low percentage of work in translation – about 5 per cent of mainstream literature is in translation – but we also have to recognise that the UK is the biggest publishing market, with Germany, in Europe. And it comes from a wide range of languages – most of it is in French of course – but it does come from a wider range of languages than in most countries. If you go to Denmark, where I'm from, you will have a much higher percentage of translations, but they will predominantly be from English.

It's about curiosity. Lawrence Venuti, the famous translation scholar, said that English publishing was xenophobic and imperialist at the same time. There is a history behind global English that we are a little bit ashamed of. But I think that is too simplistic. It's not completely untrue, but it does not account for the incredible number of publishers and translators that work in this country and the number of readers who actually do read in translation. So I don't think the problem is availability because, according to Literature Across Frontiers and the research project 'Translating the Literatures of Small European Nations', which I co-led, over the past ten years there's been a growth of sixty-nine per cent in terms of published titles. The problem is, are they being read? Who are they being read by? The biggest problem as I see it – it probably maps onto Brexit – is that there is a lack of diversity in the readers of translated literature, and it has a sort of skewed social basis. So it is very much the citizens of metropolitan areas who have access to and are being pushed to reading literatures in other languages.

KHAIRANI BAROKKA   I have 'native fluency', an interesting phrase to think of, particularly in the context of nationalism, and considering I'm an Indonesian citizen and nothing else, in both English and Indonesian, writing, reading, and performing in both, and translating as well as interpreting from Indonesian to English and vice versa. On the one hand, I adore English as an art form, but on the other, Indonesia has hundreds of languages and, as is the case around the world, an urgently dangerous language extinction rate, particularly for mainly oral languages. In a country with fewer resources due to its history of theft by Western countries, curricula are increasingly devoted to the English language to the exclusion of Indonesian and other literatures, because of the economy, and this is terrifying to me.

I wrote a poem recently called 'money for your english' for the Asian American Writers Workshop that speaks to this. Hopefully, more translation of languages within Indonesia into English and other languages will increase the viability of native languages. There is a history behind global English, as you say, that is imperialistic, as there is of Indonesian within Indonesian national

borders, but it is also the present and future. Often a notion is presented that there is only one English or Indonesian, as opposed to multiple regional dialects, usually created by imperialism, colonialism, and creative responses to them, i.e. Singlish in Singapore; or sign languages, also often disregarded as 'proper' languages.

'ABSENCE, SANCTUARY AND WEAPON'

MAROŠEVIĆ   Translation is often seen as something positive and inclusive because it makes a text available to more readers and it dissolves the boundaries between one culture and another, but I wanted to discuss its exclusive potential. Okka, you have a really nice way of describing translation as 'absence, sanctuary and weapon'. Can you explain what you mean by that?

BAROKKA   I wrote an essay for *Poetry Review* that came out this summer called 'Translation of/as Absence, Sanctuary and Weapon' which explored those ideas through two case studies. The first was one of my favourite performances of anything ever. There's this literary festival in Bali called the Ubud Writers and Readers Festival, that I've taught at a couple of times, and which is largely catered towards foreign tourists; the performance happened at the opening in a temple setting. The performer was Cok Sawitri who is a veteran performance artist and poet. She's Balinese; she's actually Balinese royalty as well as a sacred priestess. She's amazing because she's always been against the neoliberal colonisation of Bali that's been happening, including environmental damage and overdevelopment and everything. She was performing this opening performance dressed in traditional Balinese clothing and speaking in Indonesian and Balinese, but she was completely making fun of all the tourists. She was saying things like, 'You'll go back to your hotels and eat banana pancakes that we've put our snot in,' you know, and I was just so amazed. The chutzpah of her.

MAROŠEVIĆ   But the tourists just found it charming?

BAROKKA   Yes, they were clapping at the end. We were all clapping for different reasons, which was exactly the point because people who didn't speak Indonesian or Balinese were like, 'Oh this is such a wonderful traditional Balinese welcome!' and we were like, 'They don't know at all! They don't know what she's been saying!'

As a disabled artist I always try to make sure my performances are accessible, but I wondered, if that performance had been translated into sign language, which sign language would it have been translated into? BISINDO, which is the standard Indonesian sign language, or Auslan, which is the Australian sign language? But if on the programme it had said 'only translated into BISINDO', because you don't want the tourists to know what she's doing, then that would have been a tell. So I was thinking about accessibility in that sense, and what is absence for some is actually sanctuary for others, for us insiders, and even then I was both outsider and insider because I'm Indonesian but not Balinese. I have Balinese cousins and family but I don't speak that language, so I'm sure she was saying all sorts of other things that I did not understand. There were many layers to it, it was great.

'HOLDING AND AFFIRMING COMPLEXITY'

BAROKKA   The second example is my book *Indigenous Species*. It's an illustrated book and on every left-hand side I put fake flat Braille to mark a translation of absence, so that in the sighted version, as it is called, it will make the reader think, 'These pages are where the Braille should be', and to recall, 'Oh, it should be there in other books as well, but it isn't.' I was thinking about how translation of absence is not necessarily a bad thing. Sophie Collins also wrote a great essay in that same issue called 'Erasing the signs of labour under the signs of happiness: "joy" and "fidelity" as bromides in literary translation'. It's about how if we talk about translation in negative and positive terms it's very flattening, and what is negative and what is positive anyway? I'm interested in Sara Ahmed's work on being a feminist killjoy, and how she argues that being negative is seen as a bad thing, but actually when you feel things that are naturally harmful to you and you call attention to it, that's actually a good thing. I've experienced this when I've been commissioned to write about disability. I recently had someone say, 'This is quite a bitter poem, could you write one that's more positive?', but it's a protest poem, and for me protest is positive because we need change.
BRIGGS   I think what you're describing is about holding and affirming complexity. The question

was phrased as, is translation open and inclusive, or is it exclusive and exclusionary? We've just been talking about Brexit, and the way in which these questions get phrased in terms of yes or no. Are you in or are you out? Is translation a good thing or a bad thing? The phrasing of the question invites simple answers: 'Yes I'm for it' or 'I'm against it'. I think there's something about translation as an activity which holds together apparently contradictory thoughts, because we're dealing with something that is in some ways the same and in some ways different. In meaningful ways it's the same, and in very meaningful ways it's quite clearly not. And you have to be able to hold that and think with that, from that place. I think one of the things that translation offers us is that kind of mode of thinking. So the translator is, has been, historically invisible. But the translator is also extremely powerful; undervalued and yet has extraordinary determining agency. Like, both of those things. It's complicated. I think often conversations around translation are framed in this polarising way of good or bad.
BAROKKA   Which is against the project of many translators.
BRIGGS   There's something in the very nature of translation as an intellectual, creative, political project which undoes that polarising yes/no, for/against mode of phrasing questions, I think.
BAROKKA   Yeah, but those kind of questions are also embedded into the economic structures of translation – which languages are chosen for translation first or at all, as opposed to others.
BERY   Especially when you're talking about extremely unequal and diverse societies like Latin America, Asia or India. I guess it's slightly different in India because the most prominent and privileged writers tend to write in English anyway. Brazil is a very good example. The vast majority of Brazilian writers who get translated into English are white and from Sao Paulo or Rio de Janeiro or from the south – basically the wealthier parts.

ECONOMICS; INEQUALITY; COLONIALISM

MAROŠEVIĆ   Where is that decision-making happening? Who is making those decisions?
BERY   Well, it's the power structures in the culture. The big publishers are much more willing to pick up books written by well-off middle-class white Brazilians. It's no different to our society.

But when you consider what tiny percentage of Brazilian literature comes into English, it's the very tip of the iceberg of that culture, and it's going to exaggerate the inequalities that already exist within that culture. It's not that there aren't amazing projects, like *Words Without Borders*, but these are not necessarily going to make a huge impact on the wider readership. If you read *Words Without Borders* you're interested in marginal writing anyway. But the chances of, say, a poor black Brazilian from the country's interior being picked up by a big publisher is minute.

The fact that Faber, for example, published *Ghachar Ghochar* by Vivek Shanbhag, which was originally written in Kannada and not in a more widely spoken Indian language like Hindi or Bengali, was quite remarkable. In fact, that they published an Indian novel in translation from any language is remarkable when you consider how many talented Indian writers there are writing in English. So, you know, it is happening a bit more. But even then, Shanbhag is probably in a very comfortable position within Kannadiga society. In countries where inequality is extreme, we get a gross version of that inequality in the translated literature we receive from that country.

BAROKKA   I was also thinking about the legacies of colonialism, and about how much more valued the written word is over oral cultures. So for instance, my dad's Javanese and they have a very long history of epic writing and we have our own versions of the Ramayana and the Mahabharata written down in the ancient script. But my mother's side is Minangkabau and although we have a lot of contemporary writers writing in Indonesian, historically the Minang literary culture is oral. In the past storytellers would sing kaba, which are these long epic poems or stories, to people in the villages, and that's not happening so much any more.

I think there is a very colonialist line of thinking that the written word is best and proper and real literature, and if it's oral then it's somehow less than. I see that in poetry in general. I came up through performance poetry and other poets in my cohort are often like, 'Well it's not legit until it's written down.' I do think about that, especially in terms of language loss and the increasing numbers of languages that are going extinct. So many of those are oral languages—

BERY   Or languages that have a specific social purpose, like Nushu, a script from the Hunan

province in China that was used only by women, who weren't allowed to receive an education, which no man could read. The purpose of that language and the way it will be used is very specific.

ORAL CULTURE; FEMINISMS

BAROKKA   I created The 12 Acres Project with artists from the Bori Women's Economic Self-Help Group in rural Rajasthan and we recorded their stories spoken in the oral language of Vagdi, which was so great because it became a space for very feminist song-stories. I then translated them into picture books because there was a hearing-impaired member of the village who was a friend of mine. But then accessibility multiplies, right? At first I thought the picture books were for her and for that residency and space, but then kids from the school said, 'We also don't understand this language that is going extinct', and the picture books allowed them to finally understand what their mothers were singing about. It's a dying oral language, but it's also a very feminine language in the way that they use it. The songs recognised and created a very particularly female space, which is precious. I think with language extinction we're also talking about the extinction of feminisms. Which is scary.

BRIGGS   Which languages and which cultures and which literatures do we recognise as being 'of value'? And worthy of signalling, to accrue cultural capital for ourselves? And which ones do we not? One thing that really struck me, when I was still living in Paris and my son was in maternelle, was that his bilingualism – English-French bilingualism – was something that the teachers would comment on and praise. Whereas there were like ten other kids that were also bilingual.

BERY   Who spoke Arabic or West African languages...

BRIGGS   Yeah, or Chinese. And that was not something that was being affirmed.

LANGUAGE-SHAME

MAROŠEVIĆ   Rahul, you were working with kids in schools who had just come to the UK and spoke multiple languages. You've written about how schools are often filled with multilingual children and yet it's seen as a source of shame, rather than a gift.

BERY   Unless they speak French, or another

so-called high-status language. And it's much rarer that you're going to get a bilingual French kid than a bilingual Somali or Polish kid. I think there are varying levels of pride but even then it's all about fitting in. Especially if they were not born in the UK. Often they'll do anything just to be British, to be like everyone else.

BAROKKA   And the notion of 'Britishness' itself being associated with monolingualism and monoculturism is also a factor; I felt the same shame as a kid when in Western countries, and often think about all the societal factors that created that shame.

MAROŠEVIĆ   I wasn't born in the UK, and my mum was very clear that at home we would speak English. But then within the Bosnian community it was always awkward because our Serbo-Croat wasn't as good as everyone else's, so it was a choice of which language we were going to be good at. But I wanted to ask, Rahul, how you think the education system could better promote those languages that are in schools already?

BERY   I mean a lot of schools already do a really good job of it. I don't think it's necessarily the schools' fault. I think it is almost an embedded attitude, a classic immigrant situation. You come to a country, you want to better yourself, you want to fit in. Somalia's a good example in the British context. It's a country most people picture in terms of war, pirates, extremism – all these supremely negative things, grotesque exaggerations. Then also historically it's not a written language, although it has an incredible oral literary tradition. We don't really have a way of valuing that any more, even though only a few hundred years ago we had an oral literary tradition, and maybe still do in Wales and Scotland, if not so much in England.

It's a two-way thing in the sense that many primary schools do promote languages, they have initiatives like 'language of the week'. It's pretty much orthodoxy in education theory that bilingual children should continue not only to speak their mother-tongue language but to be literate in it. And it's like what you were saying, Željka, how people saw your situation in terms of a trade-off. Either you're really good at English and you're a proper British citizen, or you keep your culture but you're never going to fit in. But actually I think it's been more or less proven, from a neuroscientific level, that both languages benefit each other, and that multilingualism is almost always an advantage in terms of development.

I think we tend to think of bilingualism in terms of markets. Like, I want my kids to learn either French so they can read all these great writers, or Chinese so they can work in business in China, forgetting that most international business-men in China are much more likely to learn and operate in English than Chinese.

BAROKKA   For sure, local Indonesian languages being seen as less sophisticated and of much lesser value, and therefore deserving fewer resources, is a function of thinking in terms of markets, rather than priceless cultural value.

MAROŠEVIĆ   What about schemes like Translators in Schools and Shadow Heroes – where translators go into schools and teach translation to children?

BERY   Yeah and not necessarily to specific language groups either. It's not about, say, doing a Portuguese translation workshop with Brazilian students in Tottenham, but mixing it up. I think this is really important – having translation as a fun thing. A creative thing, not just something you do if you're amazing at languages. When you're a teenager and you read Camus or Kafka, you don't think, 'How is this an accurate reflection of the French?' You just read *The Outsider* and you're like 'Oh my god this is so amazing.' I've also heard anecdotally that children who are, say, Urdu speakers do workshops like this and think, 'Wow, I can actually translate from Urdu as well.' I've heard some children say, 'I knew you could be a translator but I presumed you had to know French, that you couldn't be a translator from Punjabi.'

STOUGAARD-NIELSEN   Well, there is some truth to that.

BERY   From a market perspective.

STOUGAARD-NIELSEN   If you want to be an interpreter, that's something else. But that does reflect reality, right? If you want to make money.

BERY   Yeah, I'm not really talking in career terms so much as in a kind of enriching activity. There is that.

'WHAT DO WE REQUIRE OF OURSELVES?'

STOUGAARD-NIELSEN   As a general thing, multilingualism doesn't really fit into schools. And I think that's the problem. Translation is going on all the time without people noticing it. Children are translating school rules for their parents who might not be fluent in English, or for the new kid from the same country. Kids are working as translators in schools without that being recognised, without the ethics behind that being understood and the possibilities that this creates in terms of intellectual development. In terms of linguistic development.

BAROKKA   Especially in London you hear so many languages being spoken every day, people are translating for family members all the time and that's very meaningful in a personal way that doesn't have to be institutionalised.

STOUGAARD-NIELSEN   But you're translating between institutions, and that's really crucial. There's a lot of skill that goes into that, it goes beyond language because children have to negotiate between different cultures: what do I want my parents to know? And it's an amazing responsibility that you give to children.

BAROKKA   It really is.

MAROŠEVIĆ   What those kids, what you are doing Okka, is also a form of care work. Children are often interpreting a whole new world for the adults in their lives because kids master the language faster.

BRIGGS   The opening question was about the Brexit mentality. But I think there is something related to that in what you're saying around the question of: What do we require of ourselves? Generally speaking, what does the British citizen, as apparently represented by our current government, require of themselves in terms of their relationship to other cultures and other languages? And I think there's a sense in which the answer is: not a lot. Because what we require is for that care work, that interpretation work, that translation work, which is live and happening all the time, to be done precisely by others who aren't 'us'. Because we assume that we can operate in English and everyone should operate in English, and, generally speaking, other European countries if they want to speak with us will operate in English. And that kind of assumption, or presumption, which is so historical, is so embedded and ingrained in the British mentality that it then leads to a failure to recognise and value and celebrate all of this activity and work that's happening all the time by others – it can't be recognised, in order for that presumption to hold.

MAROŠEVIĆ   It's the secret work that holds everything else up.

BRIGGS   Exactly, exactly. And I think there's something about that: it's not required of me to

come towards you, it's required of you to come towards me.

'YOU'RE BRITISH BUT YOU DON'T WANT TO SPEAK ENGLISH?'

BERY   This is something else I've been banging on about in my British Library role. Some people are appalled when they go to North Wales. They say, 'What? You're British but you're choosing not to speak English?' People cannot comprehend that it's not just all the immigrants who aren't speaking English, it's actually Welsh, Scottish, and even some English people who say, 'No, we don't want to speak English all the time.' It's that sheer inability to understand why you would not speak English.

BRIGGS   I'm living in the Netherlands now where there is, from my perspective, an amazing ease around bilingualism, to the point where I think English is considered a second language. It has this status where you really can operate without learning Dutch. You know, can go to the doctor and speak English. But nevertheless, I'm learning Dutch and so are my kids. And being back at the beginning with another language, it makes you very vulnerable, you feel inarticulate and stupid. Again it's the question, what do we require? We require others to come to us precisely so they are vulnerable and inarticulate and getting it wrong, and we can remain in the position of linguistic mastery. And I think one of the valuable things about translation as a practice is the way it upsets your own sense of mastery and competence. The exercise requires you to open your interest to what's different from you and to understand it. It exposes you to what you don't know in a really practical, powerful way.

STOUGAARD-NIELSEN   There is a general perception of language as being sort of homogenous. But English is a particularly good example of how that is not true. There are so many different kinds of English.

BRIGGS   Yeah, that's true.

STOUGAARD-NIELSEN   In a sense people have been reading in translation for generations in Britain because there are so many ways of writing in English. Whereas you come to a small country like Denmark, where I'm from, and everybody sounds the same because for centuries we have done away with any sort of local or regional linguistic differences in the school system. But if you go to Norway you have all these different kinds of dialects, and two different languages, so they are celebrating the idea of difference as part of their national identity. You can understand English in itself as always being in translation, particularly in a city like London, where people speak English in so many different ways, and you also find literature written in English in so many different ways. The fundamental challenge to any school system is to instil this idea into its students. That if you understand the world as being conditioned by translation, and not translation being a choice, if you see the world as being conditioned by multilingualism then it reaches into every person, even if you don't speak a second language. You are still in a culture that is multilingual and you can't choose it. It is inside of you, it's not a choice that you can make to learn a little skill.

BRIGGS   It's not a supplementary activity.

BOUNDARIES; BINARIES; NABOKOV

MAROŠEVIĆ   This leads me to my next question, which is kind of a step back. How would you all define translation? Those of you who translate from another language, what is the work that you're doing?

BRIGGS   Can I just say something in relation to what you said Jakob, about the non-homogenous nature of languages?

The first question was about whether translations into English are a good thing. For me as a reader they're a good way to understand how the things we receive as entirely novel or innovative in an English-language publishing setting, might have already been happening at the same time in Norway, or in Latin America. So there's something about the way in which translation exposes the falsity of these boundaries.

The formations of the disciplines historically, the idea that we have something called English literature, we have something called French literature, doesn't take account of the fact that the writers producing French literature have been reading English-language writers and have been informed by them. There's a cross-pollination happening at the level of the reader/writer, which doesn't pay any attention to, or isn't in any way beholden to, chronology or to the idea of there being a fixed boundary between one literary tradition and another.

STOUGAARD-NIELSEN   And that's changed as the rest of the world has, right? There are more and more writers who are writing in a different language to the one they grew up in. And that's one of the challenges to our sense of literary studies or national philologies, as we call them, because how do we deal with that? There's lots of scholarship on the literature that is travelling already. It's time to think, 'OK, if that is a condition today, was that not also the condition a hundred years ago?' And then you start finding that actually there's quite a lot of the things that we call British culture that are already in translation or born translated.

BERY   We worship writers like Joseph Conrad, Vladimir Nabokov and Samuel Beckett, who at different points chose not to write in their native languages.

MAROŠEVIĆ   I see that a lot in contemporary German fiction. You get a lot of migrants and refugees to Germany writing novels in German and then those books are translated into English, so it creates three levels of translation. And we're going to see more and more of that, especially after Germany took in so many Syrian refugees. It's going to be fascinating to see in twenty years' time what literature is coming out of Germany.

BRIGGS   But that reality is not reflected within education in the ways we uphold disciplinary boundaries and say things like, 'I'm a French scholar.' So I think that's really interesting and also kind of problematic in relation to what you were saying, Jakob, about finding ways of affirming our condition as being in translation, in cultural and linguistic translation, from the beginning – whether we're monolingual or not. How does that then get reflected and represented in our systems of learning, in the ways in which we divide the field of knowledge? I think there's a definite mismatch between those two things. It would be very exciting to think of ways of affirming the real... But then – sorry, the question is, how do you define translation?

STOUGAARD-NIELSEN   I was trying to avoid that question by answering previous ones!

MAROŠEVIĆ   Does anyone want to try answering it?

STOUGAARD-NIELSEN   I think it's probably not as interesting to ask what is translation than to ask what is the use of translation, or what is the function of translation? Language has always been filtered into different kinds of registers and geographies and cultures, so this idea of national languages being homogenised so that they can be taken wholesale and transmitted into something else, which is also wholesale, is a fallacy. In Denmark we always said, 'Oh! Everybody has to learn Danish because that is our pure national language.' But it's forty per cent German really.

BERY   And it's mutually intelligible with Swedish as well.

STOUGAARD-NIELSEN   Yeah, to a large extent it is. We can speak an interlanguage together, but there are words that we each know the other doesn't understand. That's one of the reasons why Scandinavian languages are so well-translated, they are all in the top ten of the world's most translated languages. It's not because everybody around the world loves Scandinavian literature but because within those five or six or seven nations there are translation systems in place so that when a book comes out it will first be translated into one of the other Scandinavian languages. So that region in itself is a region that is constantly in translation, before it reaches the European mainland and then finally makes it into Anglo and global American publishing.

RESPONSIBILITY AND REPRESENTATION

BRIGGS   On the other hand, I feel that within that vast field of active translation activity that we've described as being lived by our children and our neighbours all the time, I find it interesting to try to introduce and then hold to some specificity and differentiation within that vast field. I think there is something different about the live translation that could happen right now if I said, 'Could you put what I've just said into Danish?' and something else that happens in terms of its duration and attention, when I say, 'Could you put a page of mine into Danish?'. Writing about translation in my book *This Little Art* was about trying to affirm the specificity of the activity of writing a translation, in order to get at the things that Rahul was saying about its fun, creativity, pleasures, but also its particular demands and requirements and responsibilities which are configured differently to spoken translation. I don't mean that they don't share ground, but that there is a specificity to writing a translation.

So, in answer to the question about translating, I would say that I have been primarily interested in that category of written translation. But I would

also be very interested in introducing specificity around these other forms that we're talking about. Something very particular happens when we call a piece of writing a translation. When we say it's a translation, that introduces a particular invitation to read it in a certain way; it produces a relationship between this piece of writing and some kind of precedent which we don't have access to; it opens up questions of responsibility; it comes with a promise of representation.

BAROKKA   Absolutely. Translation to me is making a specific human experience understandable to a specific set of humans, and as Kate says, the Hows and Whys are very important. In Singapore's Changi Airport, an English-language bookstore has just one shelf marked 'Asian Literature', as opposed to the entire rest of the store which is presumed not to be about or from Asia, despite its location.

'WHICH FEMINISMS?'

MAROŠEVIĆ   Kate told me about a question a friend asked her which I wanted to ask all of you. Her friend asked, 'We can see what feminism can do for translation, but what can translation do for feminism?' What are the skills that you learn through translation that you can then apply to other aspects of living?

BRIGGS   I mean it's fairly obvious to me what feminism can do for translation in terms of opening up who gets to translate, what kinds of projects get translated, what we pay attention to. And for thinking about translation as a form of paying attention and affirming that something matters – highlighting that something is worth attending to and reading intimately. So that seems clear to me. Also the way that translation has historically been gendered as being a derivative, second-order feminised labour practice. So you can see why a feminist would be interested in it – and there's been fantastic feminist scholarship in translation studies. But my friend was saying, 'So yeah, that's clear, but then what can translation do for feminism and thinking about that after the fact?' It's one of those questions you get asked live and you just can't respond there and then.

I think there is something about attending to situations and circumstances which aren't yours. The most basic response would be something of that order. To say, translation asks you, it demands of you, to question your assumptions around what goes without saying, what matters, what good writing sounds like, what good thinking sounds like, what everyday circumstances are, all of those things. As a translator you're having to deal with what is common and affirmed in the world of a particular book. You have to ask, how do I register its difference? I think within feminism we need to have more of that – of attending to circumstances and lived realities and conditions of humans elsewhere in the world, and we can do that through the practice of translation. That has to be a useful thing.

BAROKKA   I would ask, which feminisms? Because not all feminisms agree with each other. I see accessibility always as translation and always, when done well, as feminist. I think that needs to be a bigger consideration, because just as kids DIY-translate for family members, members of our communities are always asking, 'Is there a sign language interpreter? Is there audio description?' And it's an art form in and of itself. So maybe we need to rethink the classification of something as translation as opposed to something as a separate art form. For instance, if you go to a museum, there's an audio tour which says things like, 'On your left you have a Manet and this is what's happening in the painting.' It's often very monotone and dry and descriptive in a way that presumes that it is an 'objective' description of reality. Actually, it's a completely different art form to describe something properly; it's a form of oral storytelling. But an audio description is rarely treated as that. I was on a panel once called 'Creative approaches to audio description' where people shared stories of really fascinating things they were doing with audio description. So for instance, a play where the audio description was basically making fun of the director, the opportunity to say things like, 'This is a really boring bit' or, 'What the hell is she doing with that acting choice?' You don't usually get that because we've been taught to perceive audio description as representing objective reality, but there's no such thing.

SINGLE MALE GENIUS

BRIGGS   I think your point relates to the de-homogenising of feminism, of feminisms precisely, or the importance of recognising the reality of competing historically defined movements and bodies of knowledge. We were talking earlier about national literatures, for example, this idea that there's something that exists that is English literature, and the way that translation is constantly pushing at and questioning that. I think that too is translation's force, it says, actually this is not something that is simply the same everywhere. It exposes fractures and differences and also surprising commonalities across different circumstances.

MAROŠEVIĆ   I'm interested in how translation does away with the traditional idea of a single male genius and allows art-making and cultural production to be recognised as a collaboration, rather than perpetuating the idea that art is made when one person sits alone in a room. How we might use the lens of translation to reconsider some of our assumptions about how art is made; how does it unsettle certain preconceptions? Also, if we stop thinking of the text as a fixed, finished thing, and something more fluid and changing, can it also help us to rethink identity?

BERY   One of the reasons I got into translation was because I really like writing, but I'm really quite lazy and not very imaginative either. So translation is a way of enjoying some of the pleasure of creative writing. And Jen Calleja, my predecessor at the British Library, was saying yesterday at an event, and I agree with her, that translating can be seen as some Dada- or Oulipo-style challenge where you have to write the exact same thing but using none of the same words. It's like writing a novel without the letter 'e' in it or something, as Georges Perec did. Jorge Luis Borges's story 'Pierre Menard, author of the Quixote' could be seen as a parable of this nature. The protagonist publishes fragments of his Quixote – which matches Cervantes's original word-for-word – but he has not just copied the text, he has, through great exertion, spontaneously reproduced it. I view translation, at least of prose, as only one step away from this. The ultimate writing under restriction.

BRIGGS   I think that's definitely true, it's a form of writing under constraint, and that's absolutely where some of its interest and potential lies. But in terms of the original question – I've been thinking a lot about this recently – I feel we're still contending so much with a specific model of what a creative life looks like. It is still so based on a gendered model of the unattached, unencumbered, mobile male which I find difficult, because my life doesn't correspond to that in any way. I don't have that mobility, I'm attached and I'm related. I think what's so interesting about translation as a model is that it's very explicit about its relationality and the fact that it derives from something else. It's attached to something else, and it arrives pointing to something other than itself, so it's not this circumscribed, original authorship, you know, that limited, closed zone. From the beginning it's open to other sources, and I find that really helpful.

COLLABORATION; DEAD AUTHORS

BAROKKA   I was just going to say, because you're a parent, you're also translating to your kids all the time, in terms of like, 'This is reality, this is how you should understand it'. I was going to ask you, Kate, what you thought the differences are between translating an author who is living and an author who has passed away, and whose estate has rights over their work? The politics and economics that go along with each scenario are two quite different things, I feel, and also the level of engagement that the author has with the translator during and afterwards also varies from situation to situation.

MAROŠEVIĆ   Kate, what was it like translating Roland Barthes?

BRIGGS   I think Okka's right to point out that with dead authors it's not collaborative in that sense of having someone to sit in a room with and ask, although I did have the opportunity to work with the editors of the French edition. But it's also very hard to talk about the conditions of translation in general terms. I'd even want to resist doing that, and to think instead about the specific, localised situation of what it was for me to translate, you know, a pre-canonised writer and his work from the late seventies, sitting in Paris in 2010. It's a particular dynamic. That work, his work, him, me, my work, my sensibility, that timeframe, that relation between French and English, it's entirely particular. And it's not the same as translating work by a contemporary, living French philosopher, or a different one; it's not the same as going from English into French. Each time – if we think about translation as being relational – those relations are configured uniquely. That specificity you're describing, it's perhaps not possible to generalise out from that to another circumstance because each pairing of language, culture, body of work to translator, historical moment to historical moment is particular.

STOUGAARD-NIELSEN   I think it's very hard to tell those two situations apart, between translating a dead author and a living one, which I think is interesting in itself because obviously in practice it must feel different to be an email away from asking an author their opinion. But not really, because if they're dead authors they're often canonical authors, so they will have a whole community of people speaking on their behalf, or they will have somebody who is responsible for their estate, so there's always a dialogue. And there's always a dialogue which can potentially go horribly wrong, like all conversations. I think dead authors are very, very loud.

VULNERABILITY; RISK

BERY   So Kate, you are the only person who has translated that volume of Barthes's lectures. But imagine if someone was like, 'Do you want to do a new translation of *Mythologies*?' I presume you would feel much more daunted by that, knowing there is—

BRIGGS   No, I think I'd feel much more excited by that! You have an existing work which has functioned and invited readers into the work of Barthes all these years, but that was made in the early seventies. I think it would be super interesting, and you'd be enabled to do something else precisely because that exists and has worked all this time. But this collaboration element – and maybe this links to parenting somehow – the analogy I found useful to think about around responsibility was: as a parent, let's say, I'm responsible for you, my child, and I can't expect you to be responsible for me because you're a baby, or a ten-year-old. There's something of that order I feel in the dynamic with translation. 'I'm responsible for you, for your work, dead person, or indeed live person, but I can't expect you to be responsible for me.' And that for me links into something about the kinds of exposure the translator contends with, or the kinds of risks, the vulnerability, you have when you've made a promise to represent the work of someone else and you've done that with rigour and seriousness.

I also think it's really important to presume that the translator has proceeded with rigour and seriousness. What it is to say, 'I represent this work, I'm responsible for this work, and however collaborative that might feel, even with a dead person's work, in the sense that your writing is informing mine, it's underneath mine, it's producing mine, I'm with you in your thinking, or I think I am.' Actually there's a certain point where there's a kind of standing alone, for, and being held accountable, rightly, for one's work. But that feels like a great risk, I know it caused me great anxiety, far more anxiety than publishing my own book under my own name. I was far more anxious about the publication of the translations than when I wasn't saying 'I'm responsible'. With my own book I'm just responsible for my own thinking, and I hold to my own thinking and we can argue about it, but I hold to it.

MAKING MISTAKES

BERY   If you publish your own writing, maybe if you're a historian you can actually get something wrong, but if you're writing a personal essay or fiction you have some poetic license. Whereas I could publish a translation and someone could say, 'This sentence is a mistake', and that's quite horrific. Not, 'I don't agree with the translator's choice' or 'This bit sounds over-literal' but 'You got it totally wrong'. I did a translation duel recently at the British Library with another translator, and I made at least one complete mistake. You know when you make a false friend mistake and I rushed it, and that was awful. I was in front of an audience, having to admit it, it wasn't something that could be brushed off as my interpretation. In Portuguese the word 'lanche' means a 'snack', but it actually comes from the English word 'lunch', so it's very easy to see that word and say lunch, but anyway, it was just a really basic error.
BAROKKA   To be fair though, they're both food. At least you weren't like 'the moon'. If you think of a translation as always being its own separate art form, which it is, it's always a new work of art.

   In my PhD now I'm looking at all these archives based on this girl who is called Annah the Javanese, in a painting by Gauguin of the same name, and her ethnicity is always different. It's always Dutch-Indonesian, Malay-Javanese, and it becomes this whole discussion of what she is phenotypically, which is very problematic in and of itself. But none of these historians correct each other because she is deemed so insignificant a person. I always think about power dynamics in terms of which mistakes are honed in on by a community of translators, and why that mistake in particular is scrutinised. What is the significance of this sentence or that passage for other people, as opposed to the example of this girl in the painting?

It doesn't really matter what colony she's from as long as she's from a colony, is part of my thesis. That's why in things as supposedly canonical as the Tate Library archives, a print of her was listed as of a Polynesian, and I had to contact an artist who had recently taken out the print, who was working on Polynesian girls, and say she's actually called Annah the Javanese, and she was like, 'Oh, I had no idea.' The Tate Library is supposedly so spot-on, but nobody could actually tell what she was because history has been translated through white men.

SUBJECTIVITY; MASTERY; DIVERSITY

MAROŠEVIĆ   Emily Wilson has done a lot of great work explaining why who translates matters. On her Twitter she often goes through choices she made when she translated *The Odyssey* and says, look at what all these men have translated this woman as being like, but actually, if you break down the language that's not how she's meant to be represented. So much rests on who is doing the looking.
BRIGGS   A decision made by a person, a subjectivity, working in a particular moment in a particular time has these determining effects which are then ongoing. It then produces conversations and further scholarship, so there is this sense that it matters a great deal when you come down on a decision as a translator, and translators, I think generally speaking, take this incredibly seriously. But I also think, at the same time, it's really valuable to affirm vulnerability. Like you said, Rahul, it was awful that in front of a crowd you weren't a master of that situation. But so much of the current discourse around translation, and about having a robust critical culture around translation, is about preserving domains of mastery. So often it reads as, 'Let's be commonsensical about this, of course there should be basic linguistic competence, you shouldn't be making that kind of mistake, oh and by the way, if it were under my watch, if I was editing this with all my years of experience, such mistakes would not happen.'

   I think it's profoundly enabling, as a translator taking her work seriously, feeling deeply anxious about it, to hear other translators speaking from a place of vulnerability and uncertainty rather than insisting, 'I've got it covered in my work.' Let's assume that we're all serious and rigorous, and we are also fallible and biased and subjective, and dealing with the ways in which our unconscious, our subjectivity, our experiences are informing the decisions we make. So I think to do what you did, Rahul, is really powerful for the young translators in the room. I think that's really, really important for them to feel enabled, to see that they too could have access to this practice which, as you said, is fun and exciting and challenging. You only get further access and diversity if you're willing to suspend a discourse of mastery for a while.

BAROKKA   Speaking of dogmatic, what you were saying made me think about translations of religious texts, and how combative that whole sphere is. I grew up Muslim and there are feminist interpretations of the Koran which I know about now but when I was little I had no idea they existed. We were supposed to just intuit, 'Well, God cares about you too.' Some of the religious teachers I had would say things like, 'This may seem a bit funny to you as a woman but trust me, it's feminist.' So often in religious translations you don't get any sense of who translated it at all.

TAKING NOTICE

BRIGGS   To go back to what you were saying earlier, Okka, about the Javanese girl whose identity didn't matter to some translators, I think therein lies such a powerful argument for diversity among translators in terms of what we are alert to. Like Emily Wilson translating *The Odyssey*, she's attending to things which would otherwise not be noticed, not count. That example is a really powerful example of why it really does matter that our translators are not all white middle-class and London-based. But that plays into further questions around the conditions of translation, practically, in terms of making a living from translation, and who is able to work so intensely, for so little money.

BERY   In *This Little Art*, Kate, you write about Helen Lowe-Porter, the translator of Thomas Mann's *The Magic Mountain*, and how one of the reasons she became a translator was because she was a housewife.

BRIGGS   It was a way of working from home.

BERY   Has translation historically been a more egalitarian profession in that sense? When women were generally in a domestic sphere, they could earn money—

BRIGGS   But that coincided with translation

being invisible, devalued and underpaid. They were doing it precisely at the time when no one cared about it.

BAROKKA   I read about a study conducted at Cornell University that showed that when more women enter any industry, the more devalued it becomes. Wages go down. It's a horrible problem.

BRIGGS   That really links to your questions at the beginning: is translation a good thing? We're celebrating translation and we're excited about translators having more visibility, and then this query appears: why do we need to bang on about translators all the time; why do they need so many prizes; why are they so thin-skinned? It's interesting to make that correlation between it being a female-dominated industry, and women attaining more visibility for their work, and then so soon the push-back of, but surely it's not that bad, they're asking for more than they deserve.

ITALICS; CHICKEN TIKKA MASALA

BAROKKA   We should just be grateful that we get a seat at the table, so to speak. Another thing I was thinking about is women's choices. I made a decision a while ago not to italicise any words that are Indonesian in my poetry, even if the poem is in English, and also to always put the glossary at the back and not as a footnote on the page. But I have been corrected, by men. They say it's traditional to italicise if a word is not English, and then I'm like, 'But I'm an Indonesian person who lives in the Western world and is using English, so what is your understanding of what is going on?'

BERY   Also, it's poetry, you can do what you want. It's like saying it's traditional to rhyme.

BAROKKA   Italicisation is also tied into exclusion and of what counts in a vocabulary, which vocabulary belongs to what language. I was foreignising words that I use as much as I use English words. How often is chicken tikka masala italicised in an English-language novel, because it's basically a British food, right?

STOUGAARD-NIELSEN   It's probably in the *OED*, though.

BAROKKA   Yes, right. That raises the question of the relationship between translators and lexicographers and what is in the *OED* and what isn't. Also though, this notion of what is transparent and what is opaque. So in *Indigenous Species* I actually use three languages: there's English, there's

Baso Minang, which is my mother's language, and there's Indonesian. I pointed out that certain phrases were a Minang phrase as opposed to Indonesian, because I want people to know that actually the book is not just in two languages. The assumption is that if you don't italicise anything else all the foreign words are from one language.

LIVED REALITY;
NEW POSSIBILITIES

BRIGGS   We were talking earlier about the kinds of writing and translation practices that might better represent our lived reality of living in multilingual environments. It's really interesting thinking about those kind of practices in relation to the way you're describing your book being written in three languages. I was just thinking about the example in *The Magic Mountain* that interested me in *This Little Art*. There's a moment where we move suddenly from German into French without it being signalled in any particular way, but the reader is expected to cope with it because a certain kind of reader in the early twentieth century actually probably could cope with it.

BERY   Even now, if you read an article in the *London Review of Books* they always just slip into French.

BRIGGS   The risk is that it excludes, but it perhaps also emphasises that we should not always expect to operate in English. What happens if there are moments of opacity and untranslated text within an ostensibly English book? What would that do in terms of the reading experience or just recognising, you know, inadequate knowledge in oneself? If not being able to access knowledge was part of the reading experience as well? It could be exciting to think of the possibilities.

WHAT EVERYBODY KNOWS

NAEL ELTOUKHY
tr. ROBIN MOGER

I'm a woman who's been through terrible trauma. I'm a woman whose first husband committed suicide, and whose second husband woke up out of a dead sleep, murdered her son, then killed himself.

Kamal woke up, killed Mahmoud, and threw himself off the balcony.

Kamal woke up, killed Mahmoud, and threw himself off the balcony. Right from the start, from the beginning of the beginning, I never blamed Kamal for killing Mahmoud. Kamal is forgiven: he had a whore for a mother and a bastard for a son, and it's at those two, bastard and whore, that the fingers of blame should be pointed. Not at Kamal, who was a victim the same way that I was a victim, and more so. The whore mother I'd already killed, but the bastard son, who'd played the lead in Mahmoud's death, what were we going to do about him?

Justice is that the killer dies, right? That's what I know. That's what everybody knows, though they might deny it.

Hours I spent on Facebook, hunting for Haytham Kamal, trying every play on the name I could think of, until I found him, and sent him a Friend request. Then nights, scrolling down his wall. I wanted to know what he was doing, where he went. Where I could find him, so I could kill him, so I could make the world more beautiful, if only for a while. Okay, I was telling myself, I'll kill him, and I'll turn myself in to the police, and I'll go to prison.

But as I was hunting Haytham on Facebook, I was also searching on Google, looking up Qanater Prison. I wanted to be fully prepared. I packed a few changes of clothes and a toothbrush. Wasn't leaving anything to chance.

When they took me to prison – when I took myself to prison – I wanted to be ready.

I'm a woman who's taken what people aren't made to take. So what do I do? Die? Can you do that? Suffer all that trauma and just make up your mind to lie down and die? Well, yes, of course you can, but what I'm saying is: that's not me.

*

If there was one person Harankash might say was her mentor, her godfather, then that person would be Amm Nagi.

Who was Amm Nagi? Amm Nagi was the first person to say the big things to her, the grown-up things. Things like, The president's selling the country. From the same district as her father, Ismail, and a fellow officer. They had joined the Staff College on the same day and become inseparable, brothers, and when each was posted to a different unit it had been Amm Nagi who'd made sure to get transferred to Cairo, to be close to Ismail. Dropping in on one another whenever they could.

Amm Nagi had attended Harankash's birth. Had loved her with all his heart. He would come round to their apartment and wouldn't let her be until he'd told her the tales of all the prophets, Adam to Mohammed. Later, it would be stories of the railway workers' strike, of strikes at the textile factories and the olive oil factories and the soap oil factories – every conceivable species of worker and factory; every type of oil – and when her father confided his ambition to see her enrolled at military secondary school, Amm Nagi had stood tall and told him, Shame on you, brother, she's a little girl. You and me? We entered the army on a whim, we didn't plan it, and your daughter's life is nothing to do with a spur-of-the-moment decision you regret yourself. You should have been a poet, after all. The girl wants a public education, so give her a public education.

And Harankash didn't forget.

*

One winter's morning Harankash put a call through to Amm Nagi. She told him she needed him urgently, something she couldn't talk about over the phone, something personal this time, something for her. And 'needed him' meaning: wanted him to do her a favour.

And Amm Nagi, who had been waiting a lifetime for Harankash to tell him that she needed him, didn't embarrass her. He said to her that whatever it was she needed and whatever it was for – anything at all, from the smallest possible thing to the biggest imaginable – she only had to turn up and she'd find it there waiting for her.

Carte blanche is what she had.

In the garden in his villa in El Marg they sat together as they always did, and she told him she hadn't been able to move from Tahrir Square. That she was still looking for an apartment away from the square, and that every day the situation was worse than the day before: that for weeks now huge battles had been breaking out, that people were swarming into the street beneath her building. They'd even climbed up to the first floor, she told him.

And me, a woman living alone. I've never experienced anything like it. I almost died of fright. I want a gun, Amm Nagi.

Amm Nagi heard her out, listening intently all the while, then he got up, went inside, and came back out carrying a handgun wrapped in reams and reams of plastic bags. He kissed it and handed it to her. Anyone comes near you, you shoot them in the arse. In the arse, you hear me?

When it was time to say goodbye they held one another tight for a long time.

*

Harankash had never lost faith in her marksmanship. Everywhere and anywhere she went she would pick out a distant target, extend her forefinger, and fire. It was just eye and finger, hardly what you'd call training, but she never, ever lost faith in herself.

Harankash was quite sure who her enemy was (it was Haytham), and she knew the means of her vengeance (the pistol), but what she did not know was the time and the place: where and how she could get a shot at Haytham and put paid to him. Her enemy gone for good. She looked carefully into all the possibilities. Obsessively stalked the child's Facebook page. She was keeping an eye out for anywhere he went alone, far from the gaze of other people, somewhere she could finish him and bring this chapter of her life to a close.

And start a new chapter in prison.

And it was right in the midst of her fevered search for the places where Haytham went that the world, once more, stopped turning. War got into people's heads and onto their social media pages and battles in and around Tahrir Square broke out afresh. From her window, Harankash looked down and saw the plates and tea glasses flying back and forth over the heads of the demonstrators, wounding wherever they fell. She saw people dropping from the impact of the glass, the fragmenting china, from the tear-gas, and amidst the flurry of defiant, bellicose posts, Haytham wrote: *I'm going to Tahrir, who's with me?* In her heart she smiled and murmured, I'm with you, sweetheart.

Harankash went out. She took up her gun, wrapped in its reams of plastic, splashed her face with Pepsi the way the demonstrators did to protect themselves from the gas, and she ran and tripped and fell and stood and ran again, and fell again, and a demonstrator trampled her arm and gave her a graze that she would live with for weeks afterwards, and this time no one told her, No chicks allowed into the square. This time no one dared call her 'chick'. But she didn't see Haytham. For three days she demonstrated, did her duty as a revolutionary and combed the square for Haytham. And couldn't find him. Her heart thumped violently all the while, but it didn't put her off her plan.

By day four Harankash was approaching the outer limits of despair. She left the gun at home and sat, face buried in her hands, on the kerb in El Qasr El Ainy, two streets away from her own front door, looking across at what had once been a petrol station and was now an empty, tarmacked lot where demonstrators gathered.

It was raining: a light rain, a sign of good things, an omen that the world would get better. And there, on the tarmacked surface of the petrol station that was a petrol station no more, she spied Haytham. When she saw him she started to shake and she ran down a side street so he wouldn't see her.

Get home, Harankash! Get the gun!

Okay! Okay! she muttered and didn't move. She was scared. Even Harankash got scared at times. Haytham was sitting in the lot smoking a cigarette with a couple of friends. You're smoking, Haytham? Little faggot. How old are you that you're smoking? She was watching him from behind a cart selling hot chickpea and tomato broth and a man hawking candy floss. She could make out bits of him, jumbled and blurred through the gaps between the customers and the bags of floss and the steam rising off the hot broth, and she was filled with hatred towards him. The hatred, rising off her heart like steam and the sound of his voice echoing in her mind: Is your son retarded? She gave a great shudder, she scraped her feet hard against the ground, and she felt a nausea, as though the hatred was climbing up from the boiling centre of her stomach's juices and she was going to flood the street and the bystanders and the cars and the demonstrators with puke, that the puke would spill over the walls and buildings of El Qasr El Ainy. During it all she never dropped her gaze from Haytham, from the broken, ghostly bits of him. And inside her was this buzzing hum, which, once a few seconds had passed, she would hear as the voice of her father, whispering to her, stubborn and insistent: Focus, Harankash.

Haytham was lighting a fresh cigarette from his previous cigarette and suddenly she saw him slump, and the tarmac was all blood and screams and chaos.

The boy beside him backed away, the people parted, then the boy ventured back and began trying to stir the body, but it didn't stir. The buzzing in Harankash's head was muddled with the short sharp cries from the pavement opposite. With blurred, unfocussed eyes she saw the little fallen body, she saw the blood, she saw the ambulance arriving, bobbing and weaving to the rhythm of the siren and the screams and the buzzing hum, and she was very frightened, and she ran home at great speed and climbed the stairs to her apartment.

The bedroom light off. Heart leaping madly in her ribcage. She opened the fridge in search of booze to calm herself, but all she found was a bottle of Pepsi. She downed it in one gulp and let off a chain of little burps, one after the other. Then she went over to the chest of drawers, took out the bundled gun and held it in her sweating palms. She threw herself onto the bed. Out loud, to herself, she said: I killed Haytham. The first words she'd uttered out loud for hours.

Now she would turn herself in to the police. She would tell them, I killed Haytham, and I killed his grandmother, and now this chapter of my life is over. Whatever you have against me, use it. She was careful not to switch on a single light, not to make a sound. Enough was the sound of her heart, which shook – or so it seemed to her – the apartment's four walls. She opened Facebook. She wanted to write something about all this, about her life which was now behind her and her fear of what was to come. So she wrote. She wrote, and deleted, and wrote and deleted, until a picture of a bleeding Haytham appeared in her feed, and beneath it the words: *Martyrdom of the child Haytham Kamal at the hands of an Interior Ministry sniper.* Then another, and with it, a comment: *The Interior are gangsters.* And another comment, this time sarcastic: *And they say the Interior can't shoot straight!*

And she smiled in her heart and thought of her father, teaching her to draw a bead on plastic plates frisbeed through the air and saying: At the right moment, Harankash, not too soon, not too late. Your heart will sense the moment and you must listen to what it tells you. Standing in front of the mirror her smile broadened. She liked the way she looked and she liked her smile. A cute thing, a cutie; she hadn't seen herself like this for years. She pointed at the image in the mirror and she said, Lord, aren't you the cutest little sniper?

*

At around two in the morning, with the photograph of the Interior's thirteen-year-old victim all over Facebook, Harankash's heart began to settle down. That was more or less when she started to think of Mahmoud. She gave herself over to the thought, to the sweet image of Mahmoud rapping on the door of her flat, and she went up to the rooftop to set up a second chair next to hers.

It was just before three when she heard knocking. She got up and opened the door.

She had wanted him to come, and he'd come.

She just stared at him, robbed of speech, and he stared back at her, unwavering, until at last, half-smiling, he said, How are you, Mummy? Harankash absorbed the shock. Didn't scream or become agitated. She was somehow ready for him, so she told herself afterwards. Had known that she would see him in the end.

Two whole minutes passed, then she smiled and said, Huh. So at last you remembered you had a mother? Call yourself a son?

His head was hatless, and he wore a filthy lined jacket. She smiled and led him inside. In he came and sat on the chair she'd put out for him. She asked him if he believed in her now, whether he realised she hadn't been unfair to him before, that she had always known who the *true* bastards were, and he replied that he had never doubted her word and asked if she had anything to drink, so she said that she'd drunk the last of the Pepsi hours before he turned up.

He was confused for a moment, then he took a hip flask from the filthy pocket of his jacket and started to drink. Sorry, he said. Mahmoud! Mahmoud, what the hell is that? She reached over and took the flask and sniffed at it, and the reek of booze, cheap and powerful, assailed her nostrils. And how old are you to be drinking this filth? It's Eid today, Mummy, today's an exception, Mahmoud said as he swigged, then he added, And Mummy? Would you mind not calling it filth? As he asked this he held her gaze and smiled, a smile as tender as the boy himself.

On the tiles that covered the roof there was a cockroach, crouched motionless some distance from them both. Harankash glanced at it then did her best to ignore it, but every now and then it seemed to swivel her way, and it made her uncomfortable. In the end she couldn't hold out any longer and she said to Mahmoud, Could you kill that cockroach over there? Mahmoud got up and went over to it, peered at it closely, and told his mother that it wasn't a cockroach, that it seemed to be a pinch of tobacco or something. Harankash got up and went over, and she bent down and touched it, and saw that, indeed, it was tobacco, a relic of her old roommate Hind – Hind, who used to roll her cigarettes and never smoked the ready-mades that Harankash preferred. How strange that the wind hadn't blown it away. Then she went back over to where they were sitting, next to the low rampart ringing the roof, and she tossed the tobacco into the street.

They watched it flutter down, flaking and scattering over El Qasr El Ainy Street: a cockroach, flying from the building and coming apart in midair. Kamal, with a pair of wings strapped on his back, soaring out from the balcony and down towards the pavement, his heart stopping before he reached the ground. The images looped through Harankash's mind, over and over, until she decided to push them away. It's a clump of tobacco, she told herself: No more and no less.

The streets below them were a shambles: the streetlights out, broken glass everywhere, demonstrators asleep and huddled in dark blankets, and the faint, acrid trace of gas hanging in the air. He watched her taking it all in and he said, Why don't we go down and take a turn in Tahrir? The offer alarmed her. Weren't they going to spend the night chatting on the roof? She said, But we can't. Tahrir's a wasteland. He gave a blithe shrug. And? Wasteland belongs to everybody. And he took a slug of the whiskey. Can I have some? she asked. He gave her the flask and she drank, and there again was the acid tang of the alcohol she'd tried that time, back when she was sleeping out on the street after the revolution, and her courage came back to her and she said, Let's go.

Down they went together, Mahmoud a touch drunk and weaving, Harankash bright and sober. They wandered through Tahrir, through the vendors selling tirmis and peanuts and tea and candy floss, and sat together in the little garden facing the Mogamma, Harankash with her arms wrapped round herself against the cold. When he saw he said, One second, and sprinted off. Two minutes later he was back with a couple of ragged blankets. Where'd you get those, Mahmoud? At first he was tongue-tied. Mumbled things like, It's nothing, and, Doesn't matter, but she insisted. He said that he'd pulled them off the sleeping body of a Salafi sheikh. You stealing from people? she said, angry now, and he answered that it wasn't like that. The Salafi sheikh was hugely fat, and the vast quantities of fat cladding his body were enough to keep him warm. Because fat's a very poor heat-conductor, Mummy. The response surprised her, and after a moment or two her anger turned to pride. You're still going to school then, Mahmoud? Yes. And you're getting good marks? Better than anyone could possibly imagine, he said, tongue thick from the booze.

And as they dozed side by side, a car came racing into the square. Harankash took fright, but Mahmoud said that it was handing out meals to the demonstrators, and he jogged off, and for a moment he was lost to sight amid the crowds thronging round the food. There were journalists, standing back and taking pictures of the scene. Suddenly a commotion broke out and the crowds round the car began drumming on the doors and the back and shouting things that Harankash couldn't make out, and then she caught sight of Mahmoud, shouting along with them, his voice quite possibly the loudest of them all. He was saying, The demonstrators aren't starving! And then he turned to face the people around him and in his reedy, child-like voice, he shouted, Think of the impression we're making, people! The vehicle sped off, fleeing its attackers, and Harankash went and caught up with Mahmoud, grabbed him by the hand and led him away. After a while, his eyes fixed on the ground, Mahmoud said, They want to show people that those demonstrators are trash, that they're starving, that they'll gnaw any bone you toss them. Then he turned to her. Mummy, do you think that the revolutionaries are starving? She stayed silent for a bit, then, hesitantly, because she didn't know whether to shout at her son or be proud of him: Are you a revolutionary, then, Mahmoud? And he didn't answer.

They went back to their patch of grass, Harankash still confused: so many words in her heart and not the first idea how to speak them to her son. And for a long time she stayed this way, stuck between speaking and not speaking, and then she made up her mind and decanted the lot: out of her heart and into his ears. I'm a revolutionary, too, you know. I'm an activist. Not a passivist. Don't go thinking that just because you go out and demonstrate you're more of an activist than I am. What I did, who'd I do it *for*? And she lowered her voice dramatically, so low that she herself couldn't hear it. You know I just murdered someone? And bit by bit, her voice began to rise: And who for? Isn't it for you, for you and all your little comrades in the revolution? Isn't it so the world might be a better place for you? The last two questions were uttered with a degree of vexation, of strain, but contrary to her expectations, Mahmoud did not flare up. He stayed silent, staring into the distance. Then he said, still staring away, Everyone's a revolutionary in their own way, Mummy. Her heart thumped with joy to hear his words, and she gave him a big hug, and she said, My darling boy! My dear Mahmoud!

About half an hour after the dawn prayer was called, as the sun began to climb up over Tahrir Square, Mahmoud informed her that he was off; that he had important things to be doing. She gripped him by the collar of his jacket and said, Don't. Don't go now, please. Can't we just celebrate a while longer? He pried her hand from the collar and took a step back – Sorry, Mummy – and walked away, calling out Bye! over his shoulder. She waited for him to change his mind and then, when she saw him determinedly disappearing from view, she swallowed back the bitterness in her heart and climbed the stairs to her apartment.

SANYA KANTAROVSKY

Something is awry in Sanya Kantarovsky's paintings. Children are snout-nosed, men grotesque and bellicose, or so floppy you could roll them up like paper – or subject them to more nefarious forms of manipulation. Kantarovsky once described his figures as having 'a fast skin', and his style owes much to satirical farce and quick characterisation of comics. There are echoes of the lascivious, soiled quality of Robert Crumb's drawings, the laconic élan of *New Yorker* cartoons, and the diabolical magical realism of Mikhail Bulgakov.

Born in Russia in 1982, Kantarovsky emigrated to the US when he was ten years old. The 2016 exhibition *Feral Neighbours* at Modern Art, London, depicted strange and sordid goings-on at an apartment building in Moscow: men with over-sized scrotums or sickly green faces, rats in boiler rooms, yellow-toothed children having their mouths probed by giant hands.

The following works are monotype prints, a method of painting on to a smooth surface then pressing the image on to paper. They are based on paintings from the exhibition *Disease of the Eyes*, Kunsthalle Basel, 2018. A variety of stock characters populate these scenes. You might find a listless Jesus hanging on the cross, or an exhausted female nude with heavy bags beneath her eyes – characters who appear to have suffered the consequences of their repetition ad nauseam. In *Oral Cavity*, Kantarovsky reprises the image of the corrupt politician. A screaming man stands at a lectern, his face contorting into a shit-stained cave. One of his hands is swollen into a monstrous fleshy mallet, cartoon flies circle his head, and down below an audience of tiny people cheer him on, like participants at a rally. The image has a genealogy that includes George Grosz's skewering of political corruption in the Weimar Republic, and Philip Guston's pillorying of the disgraced Richard Nixon. Today, when the dictatorial strongman is enjoying a resurgence, *Oral Cavity* illustrates Marx's famous aphorism that history repeats itself 'first as tragedy, then as farce'.

PLATES

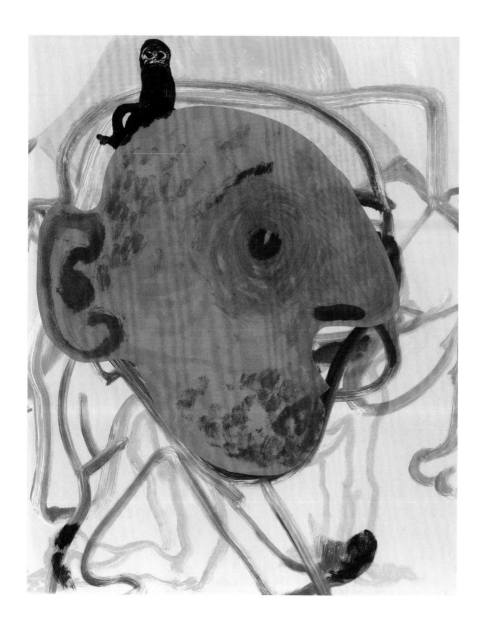

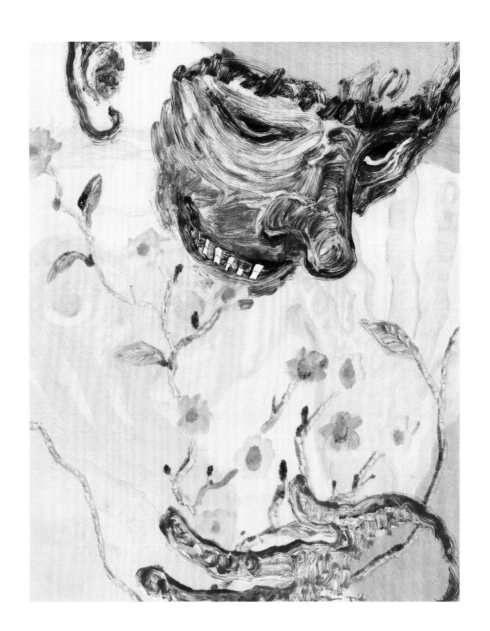

KAREN McCARTHY WOOLF

POETRY

A CERTAIN HOUR
After the Amen Break

Four and a half   inches, five, tops
black satin spaghetti strap

platforms   more like tagliatelle
they were barely

elegant
worn before jungle got intelligent

and I need your lovin', like the sunshine

in the basement at Big John's
                          East Side Diner
down Kingsland Road
                  racing mini-cab drivers

vodka and nail polish were the only things
                      in the fridge
                      we did a lot of

everything
in the back of limos,
          on the ceramic cistern lid

and I need your lovin'...

the truth is – try the podium
            if you want a confession

cos I need your lovin', like the sunshine//

it's almost impossible to remember
            easier to recall a summer
            cracked by a storm in September

cos everybody loves the sunshine
      folks get brown in the —

all sunny days are splintered/it's
something to do
/with the light   a strobe

flickering through trees
on an avenue/ in France

do you remember the time?
don't you remember
handing in your own phone
when you found it on the floor
with a cracked screen
because *your* phone wasn't...

in the sunshine, just bees and things and flowers

we were all broken
but only in the way that everyone
has a little brown seam

     running through

in the sunshine...

O discotheques, I drown among your husky broken
truth in summer's *sentences*
the truth is
over, it's nearly November

on the dancefloor, next to the speaker
men roll spliffs, serious as priests
as bass vibrates

& yes, shades are almost always appropriate
after a certain hour

OF TREES & OTHER FRAGMENTS

— they all have names, *Willow*, *Cedar*, *Oak*, *Elm*...
              mine is down a darker track
red pine shaved to skin-thick tiles

         Waterfall, by the waterfall, where spirits of the stream
race and dive from rocks, hold a small
child under —

one evening at dusk we mistake
a charred tree stump
— for a giant Man, with legs
         hidden in the brush

On Widbey Island
                        startled by a hummingbird
         I'm jumpy as a rabbit
the paths are tunnels and there's an axe
         struck deep

Mornings, at the retreat
         it's picking punnets
of sharp red strawberries, feeding rare-breed ducks
         rows of peas and chard

Victoria, dark-skinned and gamine, among candyfloss roses
and poppies, with her scarlet jumper
         and wicker basket —
she skips, almost
back to her angular, Swiss-style chalet
in a clearing, after dinner: Victoria in her little red...

*

you need to know that I don't
like
shadows and
         unidentified —
always being one step behind, behind...

*

      Jack's text says our cat
was sheltering under the mosaic table
from two jays

             I'm in Pike Place and witness
a crow attack, a blonde is dive bombed, then one more

— Is there any other language we understand?

*

In Warsaw E Annie Proulx
      writes me a note, To Karen, poet of trees, and climate change
and music, What are trees?

*

Last night Ed and I went for a walk in the dark with the moon, round
to the clearing. Last night Ed and I went for a walk,
it was dark, there was moonlight. He knew his way, in the dark,
along and off the path
      — When we get there, I slip my arm
around the rough-barked, slender waist of a young oak,
so companionable, and surprisingly warm
          my fingers trace
adolescent names scarred into the trunk, a wonky
heart

*

At the reading I tell everyone *that horse chestnut was my friend*

*

a tree is a complex being
      that has relationships
      with soil, and air, and – Jack reminds me,
mycaelia
      as well as other trees'
      roots and branches
      and insects, with teeth

when thirsty a tree emits a
      noise, high and fast
      audible to humankind when slowed down a thousand times

a tree must
      deal with many teeth

a tree is a mass
      of tentacles in a sea of leaves

    *

In the meeting we discuss a moment in Chapter 3, after
Orlando marries
when she can't physically write:
we don't need to hear the poem, it doesn't exist, the poem
is called The Oak Tree.
              It's a constant,
a companion, each era an annual, concentric ring cycle.
We know
we musn't write The Oak Tree. Not the poem. The tree
will find other ways to speak.
Surely we will welcome
the oak?

    *

Are you wearing Eau d'Lancôme? the woman
with the long-haired
Alsatian asks. Everyone has a dog. There are no women walking
in the woods without a dog. All the walkers are women.
Don't you have a dog?

    *

This is how you learn to stay alive —
      sunlight streaming
through branches —
all young girls must remain
      alert. In the holly thicket, the Princess
from *Frozen* is deflated on a punctured balloon

other debris includes a red and white remnant
of crime scene tape

    *

And then a breeze at last
   prompting leaf fall
   loud as fire
my youth flickering on and
off like
spiders' silk spinning in the sun
   among collapsed
fences, rotting stumps more than two
   centuries wide
a tiny, two-leaved seedling
pushing up

   O little seedling
you leave a deep and buried sorrow
even dancing can't derail

*

driftwood: great lobster claws
of rootlessness,
   whole palms, adrift and smoothed

what's wrong with roots? the wood asks

if trees were fully animate, surely they'd reach
down and squeeze
until we gushed like Sicilian oranges?

 *

Yoga, under the ash and weeping willow
staring up into the canopy

   ash an unlikely synonym for green, verdant
against rare uninterrupted blue
no sign of die back
or other climactic disasters, two fat-breasted wood pigeons
roosting and quiet

and I tell the story of how
I wasn't called Willow in the end, how
willow's chandelier teardrop drama
is overshadowed by its capacity for vigour
however hard you cut back

*

Jamaica, finally:
      at Devon House
      a whole class
      gathers, chitter-chattering, under a fruiting mango
          that reminds me of a tree at the hub
      of a village I passed through in Mozambique
      on the way to catch a ferry, its voluminous shade encompassing
          at least four generations, three motorbikes
          and a Vodacom vendor

*

The article describes
          the currently inexplicable
and multiple deaths of a dozen ancient baobabs
      some older than Christ

              Thirst is a possible factor

*

Trees don't need to move
      to exact revenge, leave that to the crows

trees are now you see me, now you ...
a long drawn-out, involuntary retreat
      that ends in our asphyxiation

Meanwhile, give thanks for Sandalwood and Frankincense!

*

Can a fragment ever be complete —?

      Love shook my heart,
      Like the wind on the mountain
      Troubling the oak-trees

*

04.44
and I think of the bamboo in the hills
by Glengloffe
how the grove is many-stranded yet moves as one

and I think of Moxy
bamboo carver on the beach
outside the orthodoxies of the all-inclusive
who carves cups from the stems
with a Stanley knife, as well as
bongs and an instrument similar to a didgeridoo

       there's something hypnotic as curls of
green fall down onto white
sand, his hands worn, weathered
still steady – *no* he answers, *I never left Jamaica*

*

driftwood   a horizon of
      stars and stripes, flagpole after flagpole
one flagless, where a bald eagle perches

Useless Bay   shallow and
          private, the water clear, the shoreline
littered with natural debris: for once a lack of plastic
     (so many billionaires own here)

      whole trees uprooted, bark stripped and polished
to a grey sheen, smoother than pebbles, squid-like
suckers groping cool air
driftwood/
     floating out to the ocean/ driftwood,
bleached by the sun, whittled —

INTERVIEW ANTHEA HAMILTON

It was unseasonably warm on the late September morning I met Anthea Hamilton, but inside her south London studio the two of us sat close together by a small heater. *That deep-bone studio chill*, we would say, warming up outside in the sun afterwards, yet over the three hours during which we spoke I didn't really feel it. Hamilton exudes a genial warmth, while also maintaining a sense of thoughtful and articulate calm.

Hamilton is perhaps best known for her 2016 Turner Prize installation, in which she exhibited, among other things, *Project for Door (After Gaetano Pesce)* (2015): a giant pair of buttocks bursting through a brick wall. Visitor selfies abounded, and the popular press's interpretations of the piece waxed and waned, often neglecting its specific origins – the buttocks are based on an unrealised project of 1972, by the Italian artist, architect and designer Gaetano Pesce, who proposed it as an entrance to a New York skyscraper.

To focus on the obvious in Hamilton's work is to miss the point entirely. The artist orchestrates big statements that catch the attention, so that, as she puts it, *something else can happen*. Something else, like the altering and making strange of exhibition spaces. For her solo show, *Sorry I'm Late*, at Firstsite, Colchester, in 2012, she covered the walls and floor in eye-popping chromo blue; for *The Squash* (2018), she coated Tate Britain's Duveen galleries wall-to-wall in immaculate white tiles. Materials and images are also fused in unexpected ways – you might find stills of John Travolta's face taken from *Saturday Night Fever* (1978), for example, printed on Venetian blinds, across a wall, or on a kimono – producing jarring and beguiling connections that facilitate different ways of looking, seeing and thinking.

Despite Hamilton's disavowal during our interview of the idea of having too much 'stuff', I found her studio filled with it. Fragments of materials and objects scattered across tables and attached to walls conjured various aspects of her work: scraps of fabric, high-heeled boots, lichen, a large poster for the Secession museum in Vienna, where she had recently finished installing her solo exhibition, *The New Life*. In perhaps an extreme logical extension of the grid motif employed via white tiles in *The Squash*, Hamilton covered Secession's austere walls with tartan, and placed within them a spare arrangement of mannequins, food objects and soft sculptures of butterflies and moths.

I really trust my eye, she told me, and I can see why. Throughout our conversation, her process of testing and probing materials, turning ideas upside down, became evident. *What was I looking at?*; *Who was I talking to?* and *What was I surrounded by?*, she repeated at various junctures – a testament to the close looking and critical thinking that underpin her work.

Transcribing the interview took a few days and I told Hamilton that it felt like I was hanging out with her all the time, but not in a creepy way. (In her typically generous manner, she replied, *It does sound a bit creepy, but that is OK!*) We spoke about *The Squash*, Daniel Day-Lewis, time, ageing, bodies, Bollywood, Jamiroquai, Arthur Jafa, institutional methodologies, cultural appropriation, the power of misunderstanding, romance, the devotional, and more, some of which is preserved here.   EMILY LABARGE

TWR   In your work the body is often made strange or exaggerated; it is protean. Your Perspex *Leg Chairs* (2010–2015), for instance, are transparent legs that hinge open, with seats placed between the thighs. We also see things from oblique angles, or from behind, as in *Project for Door (after Gaetano Pesce)*, first shown as part of *Lichen! Libido! Chastity!* (2015–2016), your solo exhibition at SculptureCenter, New York, and again at the Turner Prize (2016).

AH   In a practical, maybe self-protective way, I'm interested in ways of presenting a body that are non-expressive, that don't reveal what or who it is: a body that can assert itself as a body rather than the cultural signifiers that might go with it. Usually it has been an identifiable female body. Perhaps age, or any other type of status, isn't given away. Often I am trying to convey the attitude of an image, so with *Project for Door*, it was about a fuck you: this ridiculous, comic, crass, why not? In Pier Paolo Pasolini's film *Canterbury Tales* (1972), there's a scene where someone sticks their ass out the window and a poker goes up it, and the film ends with loads of corrupt priests coming out of the devil's backside. I think Gaetano took the image from a medieval painting where someone is holding their bum cheeks open, so there's a lineage to it, it's a sensibility. It's a serious thing to me.

The idea of the protean body is really nice. My understanding of my body is also changing, which is interesting, and I can't just assign it to having had a kid. It's also to do with being busier, and because my head is connected to my computer. All you can do is bring your body with you and hope your mind keeps up. I'm less physical as a person than I used to be. I'm interested in that 'not-young' body, and I'm trying to understand the romance of the inorganic. I think about what happens out in space, or in a volcano, or on rock formations, and it's wild. In rehearsals for *The Squash*, a phrase came up: a vegetable doesn't have a front or a back. It's a body in the round. It might move in order to respond to light, but it doesn't know what it's doing, whereas mammals have a front and a back.

TWR   *The Squash* (2018), at Tate Britain, is the most recent work of yours I've seen. You covered the walls of the Duveen Galleries in white tiles that were also used to construct plinths, basins and platforms throughout the space. Some displayed works from Tate's permanent collection; others were alternately occupied by a performer who moves through the galleries on daily rotation, wearing a large squash construction that covers his or her entire head. What were the responses of the performers?

AH   I think it's so mad for them that they were kind of screwed up by it. They all have different ways of preparing. Some of them begin switching into their Squash-mode the evening before. They're on the bus, travelling to the museum, and it's already happening: they're transitioning into this other sentience. Some of the performers like to interact more, some of them are trained ballet dancers who really take it as a job. I like that the audience doesn't get the same thing twice. No one can have the same experience and say *I've seen it*. That's why there's a range of costumes and a range of performers: the permutations are high. The performers are really covered up, and I like that sometimes you might see a piece of jewellery or what skin tone someone's hand is, you might get a hint of what type of body is in there.

There's an ownership people feel within the Tate. Something happens within a museum that makes it seem like things are unreal. You see people push or touch stuff, as though they can't believe that they are real themselves, that they have this capacity in front of an object. Even if a performer is within earshot, people think that because they have this thing on their head, obscuring the face, they can't hear. One of the performers told me about a group of schoolgirls trying to figure out the gender of the person they were looking at. They were split 50/50 over it, then one schoolgirl managed to turn everyone. She was like, 'Look at its knees, those are male knees.' And everyone was like, 'True, true.' And the performer inside was thinking, *what*? Not being able to respond in the moment is difficult. I briefed them, *if someone is giving you too much hassle, just take the head off*. I think that happened once. There was no obligation to perform for anyone.

TWR   What was it like making work for the Duveen Galleries?

AH   It's not an easy space, but it's not the size that's the problem, it's that it's in the middle of Tate Britain. Formally, the space plays lots of neoclassical games of architecture. It's really tall. It pretends it's grand, but it's not that big. It's like walking into a cathedral. The light in there is really beautiful, which is something that struck me. When I'm working on something there are little

things that become points of focus, and I wanted
people to look at the ceiling, the walls. When the
floor is dark, as it usually is, it draws you to it. It
pulls your body into a smallness, making the rest
of the space seem really big. I wanted my work to
feel like it was liberated from all that – so that the
floor and the ceiling and the light were part of the
work. I wanted it to have a totality, as if everything
was actually in the same state, all one mass, one
volume. I wanted to take ownership of this, rather
than to feel like I was prey to the scale of it.

TWR   I'm interested in your description of
materials being different but of the same state. For
the exhibition *Lichen! Libido! Chastity!*, you covered
portions of the SculptureCenter's extant brick
walls with painted facsimile bricks. *The Squash* is
also an exercise in perspective, the tiles evocative
of environments outside of the museum – a
swimming pool, a postmodern design installation,
a computer generated interior, a Constructivist
theatre set, and so on. It seems like you are
harnessing multiple images in one image,
different materials in one material.
AH   I've always been interested in how to be
economical, which flows both ways. I used to make
a lot of things. I had a more handmade, sculptural
process, and details within the work would hint
at codes that could be read outside of themselves.
In a practical way I just got fed up with having
too much stuff. And when you consider the space
as an object, big or small or difficult or whatever,
it becomes equivalent to a single sculpture. It puts

everything on a level plane, even though you may
experience things physically at different scales.

TWR   It strikes me that the idea of each com-
ponent being an equal part of the whole might
relate to the idea of collaboration. What were the
collaborative processes involved in making *The
Squash*?
AH   My role was holding onto the ship, holding
onto the sensation that I wanted the piece to have.
I worked with a movement director called
Delphine Gaborit, who I met through a performance work I did at the Serpentine [*Grasses*, 2016],
and she was able to grasp what I never seemed
to be able to articulate in curatorial meetings
when asked what I was going to make, or how
a performer would behave. In our first project
meeting I shared with her a mood board of images
that were key to the project, and she put into
words all of the things I had been holding onto
about what the work was. As someone who works
through physical movement, she knew *The Squash*
was not about research, but about movement and
the physicality of a person within a space.
   As an artist I tend to be a bit too slow, I often
find myself behind deadlines. Institutions take
months to make decisions. I was interested in these
different speeds, and I thought of fashion as a warp
speed. When my daughter was born, in the lead-up
to the SculptureCenter exhibition, in the pockets
of free time I had I spent a lot of time looking
at catwalk shows, which are a wave of productivity. Everything is squeezed into a ten-minute

explosion. I also worked with Jonathan Anderson [creative director of Loewe fashion house],who brought another speed. Collaborating with him and his atelier to realise the costumes I had designed was the most fun part of the project for me. Everything else was slow and heavy, but there were two days when I did the drawings for all of the costumes. I wanted the performers to look amazing, to be more dazzling to look at than the Tate, than Henry Moore, than loads of tiles, than the collection. I wanted them to be the best thing in there. I felt like we were in a transitional space, so we could make our own fun. I made the work totally for myself and those I care about. I'm not sure that people have responded to it in the way it was offered, which I knew would be the case.

TWR   What do you mean?
AH   The performer can't really see what's going on because of the headpiece, so they're having a very internal, private experience. Sometimes there are moments of interaction that I think have been really amazing for them, but mostly it's quite solitary. How do you deal with your own boredom? How can you think about being a vegetable for a day, and does it do something to you? It was made for this idea of personal endurance, which means that the people observing it are irrelevant. Maybe it would be of interest for other people who have had to endure something. Which is perhaps everyone. I thought it was key to have works from the collection in there, but as formal decoration, as a means to distract or punctuate or send someone off around a corner.

All of that stuff is purely a means by which to have something else occur. Could one person be in that room for that long, and what would need to happen in the space to enable that person to be there in a safe way? How much would you have to render for someone to be there? That was the task.

TWR   Across your work there is an interest in utopias and collectivity, what we might consider attempts at finding a 'shared language', or an alternative mode of existing within the world. How does this affect the way you work with materials and sources?
AH   I'm interested in the 1960s and 70s, because it was a recent time that was trying to assert a utopia. That was the cultural moment. When I spotted the picture of the squash character [a photograph that documents *8 Clear Places (squash)*,

(1960), a dance piece by US artist Erick Hawkins], it spoke to that era. I should be clear that there's some personal background to the image. When it came to doing the press text for *The Squash* I wanted to keep it factual, because I didn't think an institution would handle me discussing something autobiographical or personal in a sensitive way. But I didn't have enough facts. The Hawkins image is something I photocopied from a book when I was a student at the Royal College of Art. I had missed the caption on the photocopy plate, so I couldn't retrace it, I couldn't relocate the book, and no one I knew was able to help me identify the image. I only found out after the show that it was part of an Erick Hawkins dance work. His performance and ideology aren't part of *The Squash*, though perhaps it relates to my interest in utopias.

My question is, how was the identity of a counter-culture or a utopia in the West constructed? That's where it gets more complicated. That's where I question this idea of what research is, because my research is all bound by my education within the British system, and to me that seems skewed and tightly edited. It's also where I'm out of my depth. I've become really sceptical and unsure of who I am, what I am. Hawkins had taken that figure from Native American traditions, this loops back to my suspicion of the post-psychedelic utopian period in which he was working. I didn't know until after the opening that there even was an Erick Hawkins. I'm dealing with the vastness of my ignorance. No one I was working with had any idea either. There was just a void. Which makes me wonder: visually, who was I speaking to with this piece? What were the terms?

TWR   We're living in a specific moment in which there are myriad complex conversations about images. What use is appropriate or right? Where do we understand that the meaning of an image resides, and is it totally, only, in its politics? Can something be formative without having been fully understood?
AH   It is a question of ethics, isn't it? I'm interested in ancient Kabuki theatre. I know I have no access to it, and I'm not trying to gain any access to, or ownership of, it. What I'm dealing with is the way I'm completely blocked out of it and how I feel about being on the outside. From Kabuki theatre, the kimono rose to the top as the cultural, signifying object that I could take to represent how I felt about the experience of looking at ancient

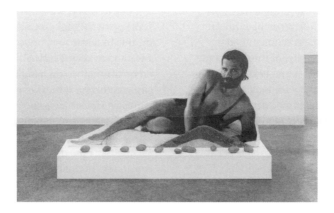

Japanese theatre. Formally, it was a kind of template in which I could combine different images or materials. It has its own iconography, autonomy, it's its own fixed thing. I hope I'm clear that it's not just something I think is cool. I guess that's why I feel unsure about the reinterpretation of the Hawkins image. Because I didn't have complete access to its source I could not accurately ask myself why I was interested in that image, like I did with Kabuki. It was more practical.

I haven't figured out how to speak autobiographically. I didn't have a really strange childhood, but the childhood I had shaped the way I perceive things. As a child I used to stay up late and watch things I shouldn't have seen. There was one season on Channel 4 that showed lots of banned, hardcore sexual and political content that I just took as adulthood. I knew it must be special, because it had been censored. So I saw Vanessa Redgrave in Ken Russell's film *The Devils* (1971), the scene in which she's masturbating with the crucifix, and I was just like, *OK*. I went to a Catholic school, so it's like, *uh-huh, OK, got it*. So much of *The Devils*, particularly the scenes with the nuns, takes place within a stark, tiled room that is like a postmodern apse. That filmic reference is where the idea for using tiles in *The Squash* actually comes from. The beauty of Redgrave, Oliver Reed, passion, lust, revolution. It educated me, and pricked my interest in postmodern design, leading me to work by people like Jean-Pierre Raynaud and [conceptual Italian architecture firm] Superstudio.

TWR   After being immersed in a long and specific commission for Tate Britain, you installed the exhibition *The New Life* at Secession in Vienna in Autumn 2018, for which you covered the gallery walls in tartan...

AH   Secession is dazzlingly beautiful – it's always been on my hit-list of where to do a show – and was built as a decadent kind of 'screw you' to the rest of the city. I've never really been able to make work in a white cube. I feel like it's a place of the intelligentsia, and that my work doesn't function in that way. I'm not downplaying myself, but I feel like my knowledge is much more held within me. I tried to enjoy the idea of making the show in this kind of temple, but all the sculptural works I planned were too *nice*. It took a long time to realise I didn't have to uphold the image of the space as a white room, because it exists anyway, whether you cover the walls or not, it's always speaking of its own image.

At that time I was thinking about graffiti, because it was all around me on the streets of my neighbourhood, and finding its calligraphic qualities quite beautiful. At one point I wondered if I could graffiti the Secession, but that seemed a really phoney gesture. I've never tagged anything in my life, it's another culture and I wouldn't know what I was getting into. I decided to run wild with the grid motif and take it to a tartan. So the space has a tartan interior, based on the pattern of the Hamilton clan. There was a syntactical confusion about what it was: someone thought that I had designed a tartan and called it Hamilton, and someone else was like, *oh, the musical*. I was like, *uh, no*. There's the knowledge that had my name been MacDonald, McLellan, etc. it would have been a different design. It's like me tagging my name everywhere, but it's also not biologically my surname either, it's this applied name that got attached to my father's family somewhere along the way. It was a way of asserting myself in the room, but also knowing that it wasn't possible to assert myself at Secession by claiming my name. I'm happy that the tartan was really garish, it was a full-on eyesore.

TWR Your practice engages in its own kind of intelligence: an internal logic that is based on different ways of connecting things – looking for the deep text of an idea or an object, to see what resonates. I'm thinking about *Anthea Hamilton Reimagines Kettle's Yard* (2016), in which you selected various pieces from Kettle's Yard – Jim and Helen Ede's twentieth-century art collection, installed in their Cambridge home-cum-public-gallery – as a starting point in order to make something new. For example, you made a kimono (*British Grasses Kimono*, 2015), printed with images of British grasses taken from photographs by botanist-photographer Roger Phillips, whose book you found in a local lending library.

AH I'm always trying to train my eye. Kettle's Yard is a very performative experience; the house is completely structured and choreographed. You'll be in there with thirty other people. It's clever how many people are allowed in at once. It's always a few too many which means you have to look at detail, you never really get an overview. If someone else is standing in front of the Miro, then you look at the cider press, an experience completely constructed by the curator Jim Ede. There's an emphasis on natural beauty and communing with nature, so works of art are carefully installed alongside collections of stones, plants or other organic materials. The density of the space means everyone can have their own particular amazing experience – it's all been set up. That's the thing *I* feel about it. I told the director that Kettle's Yard is like a state of mind, and he took it as a compliment. But I was like, *no, this place is kind of crazy!* It's didactic, it's telling you how to feel about things, sending you into raptures about stones. It's bossy. I wanted to see what it would mean for me to inhabit that kind of British domestic interior, one very different from the type of space that I grew up in. I have the feeling Kettle's Yard speaks the language of upper-middle-class British culture.

TWR In the past you have said you sometimes think of one particular person when you are making something – that it's a devotional activity. Is there something romantic, or interested in pleasure, in this one-to-one mode of looking or making?

AH Romantic can apply. It is so egotistical to think that your work can speak to the masses. It's just more precise if you can focus on one person, or one situation. The first time I ever did a solo exhibition, in 2005, the gallery floor was quite ugly. I found the female co-director of that space amazing. I hadn't met that type of woman before – wealthy, incredibly beautiful, charming, could wear high heels all day – I just hadn't come across that in life. So I decided to kill two birds with one stone. I tiled the floor so I wouldn't have to put my work on the existing floor, and also because she wore high heels, so the tiles gave her her own mini soundtrack. When she walked through the show she got this 'click click click' – it was for her. I also did a show for a gallery with a director who had very fair hair and very white skin, who always wore light-toned clothes. I chose to paint that space blue so he would always look amazing in front of it – he'd really pop.

The work at Tate was driven by my own interests, but that was more like flirting, or batting my eyelids, being romantically suggestive as a process – things I also see as devotional. I had an experience in Lyon in 2015 when I went to install work for the Biennial. It was the first time I had been away from my child, who was still a baby at the time, so it was the first time I had my body back to myself. I felt incredibly heightened, I was hormonal from all the post-pregnancy chemicals. It was really hot and super sensuous, and I was on my own and I didn't really speak to anyone, so I was hyper-stimulated by everything. I was on the way to meet my friend for dinner, and I was walking along by the river in the tall grasses, and it was an amazing, psychedelic experience. Then all of a sudden I had a flash of reality. Where am I? Is this dangerous? For the sake of stimulation, how long is it going to take me to walk there? Am I late? Am I lost? I just had to go with it. It was like when you go to a performance and you're thinking, *oh damn, I don't know how long this is going to last*, and time becomes quite elastic – you enter the time of the performance.

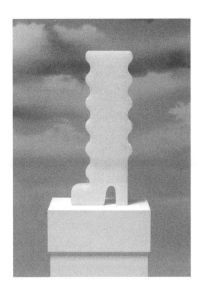

TWR   I can see a collection of lichen scattered across the table behind me here in your studio. In the exhibition *Lichen! Libido! Chastity!,* you displayed a platform boot that appears to sprout lichen and algae. Were you thinking about the temporality contained within the idea of vegetation and growth – that natural forms both generate and contain layers and strata of time?

AH   Definitely. Lichen doesn't care about us. That's what I really like about it: its independence, its lack of regard for the human. That it just takes its own time and does things in its own way. That it has its own grace, that grace is something you can't acquire, it's something you have. You are born with grace. Lichen is also tied up with defiance, it asserts its own way and what it's asserting isn't accessible to us. We can only regard it for its image. I have a recurring interest in how I process nature in my work – even if I take a bit of lichen, or a dried flower, and stick it on something. In the show at the Secession there are butterflies, but they are digitally printed onto polyester fabric. It's not about artifice, but all the channels through which I consider something to be processed.

TWR   Most plants are cellularly far more complex than animals. People talk about nature being cruel or kind, or landscapes being unforgiving – but nature obviously doesn't care that we're here. Which is not to say that we don't have an effect on it.

AH   Absolutely. That's really present at somewhere like Kettle's Yard, which seems to be presenting wildness, or man communing with nature, but it's not. There's a phoniness to the way natural forms are staged alongside the art objects in the collection: as if humanity could be contained within a single seedpod. It also has to do with how I grew up. I find *The Squash* project funny, because my mum's garden is full of squashes and courgettes and twining vines, those are the things that she grows. She's the source of everything. They had a garden at Tate this summer in response to the commission, and if she were to see it, she'd be like, 'this is *not* the way to grow it, this is completely rubbish.' There's a lived experience of how to do something, and then there's the museum, explained version of how to do something for the purposes of education. There's a directness that comes from being good with one's hands and enjoying doing it, rather than presenting enjoyment. But I guess it was a good summer for growing vegetables. Nice and hot.

E. L.,
September 2018

WORKS

PLATES

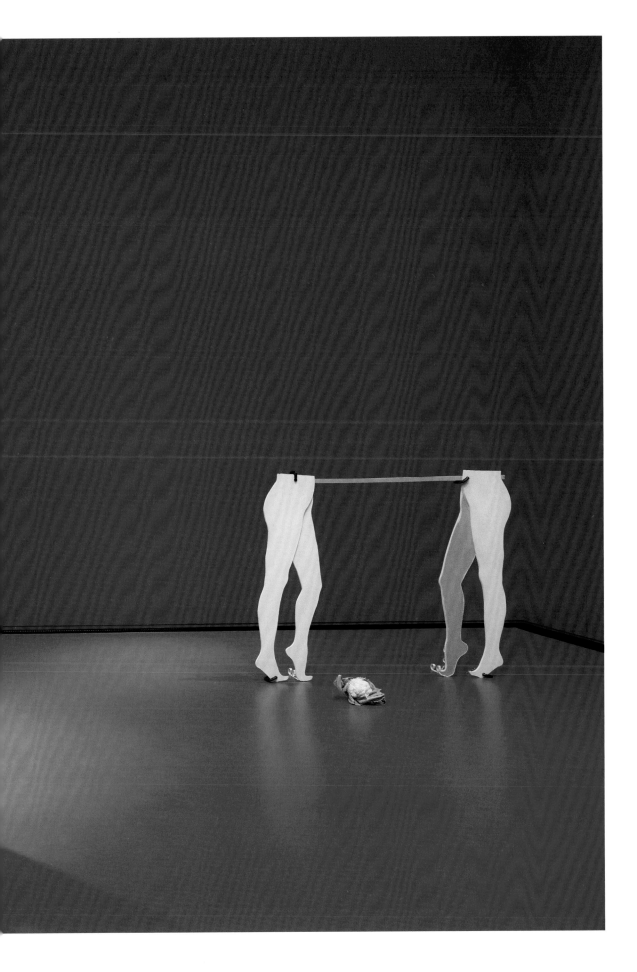

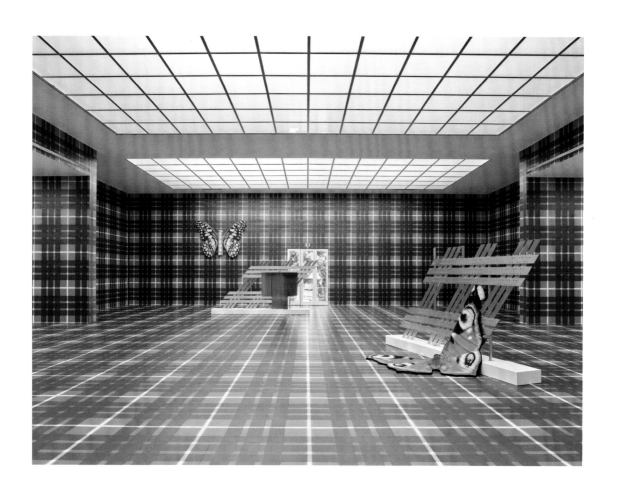

N J STALLARD

POETRY

THE BARBARA HEPWORTH BLUES

At the bottom of the garden, my mother and a woman
dressed like Barbara Hepworth argue over a sculpture of my birth,

if the bronze plinth should be horizontal or vertical,
the right shade of blue for the umbilical cord.

Hepworth adds a curl of hair with a toothbrush,
pats down the clay like a pony.

My mother sticks her chisel in, disappointed
in the arrangement of her legs, if she had her way

the sculpture would include a dancing fountain and hum
like a refrigerator, full of roses, a sundial and a coat of arms,

her snacks, soft drinks and wine. Instead the sculpture stands
in the April shadows of overgrown gorse,

one arm in the air like the chimney of the defunct
engine house where my father

worked in the summer of '85, where copper wires crawled in
beneath the sea – no messages.

But what about the father? Hepworth asks.
Oh, he wasn't involved, my mother says.

Hepworth rolls her eyes, the whites of her eyeballs
like a cliff face, the grey of her overalls

like a gun. She begins to sing:
Don't turn your back on me, baby.

Blues like the sulky one in a rainbow.
Blues like your favourite moon.

With so many conflicting opinions, a therapist
had warned the sculpture of my birth of this moment

and offered some advice: be lucid.
Talk to the older generations as if talking to the sea.

Keep a list of all their errors, like those lists
you'll keep of all the things you eat while falling in love:

roast beef, feta cheese, champagne bon bons, shish taouk,
french fries and wild grass.

Keep a list of all the places where you'll no longer have to be a sculpture
or a birth: the backseat of a servees on Rue Sursock,

a minibus across the Asian Minor,
the heart-shaped swimming pool of Le Club Militaire.

Even Hepworth will not be able to capture the light as it falls
over your face on a Red Sea bottomless boat —

the fishes kissing the glass, the moon flirting with the sky,
only hinting at its evening plans.

My mother interrupts: *Aren't the blues a bit obvious?*
The woman who once refused a pedicure

on her wedding day – who said if she wanted her toenails
in a different colour she'd slam them in the car door.

Blues like the indoors with the outside coming at you with a chisel.
Blues like your favourite ocean.

Hepworth sighs and dusts down her overalls, abandons the sculpture,
walks up the garden path, retires for the day.

And in the evening's distance, wild gorse rattles against
the windows of a passing train.

BOAT PARTY

What myth is this? The river blurts
and shudders through yet another
century, a brown thread
unspooling from the mouth of the Aegean
to the teeth of the Black Sea.

Except this river is not
a river, it's a strait.

The strait where Genoese soldiers once slept upright
in chilled, stone forts.

The strait where star-spangled bishops still commit
a yearly crucifix,
chucked into the depths and fetched
out by pilgrims
among the braindead, hormone-hard pike.

The strait where Io, transformed into a cow
and condemned to wander the Earth,
swam from bank to bank
to escape the gladflies.

Flies regather now, era-less and inky-faces
kiss the beer bottles,
and dance in right angles
above the sunbathing bodies
of a boat party
where foreign correspondents
take their first day off in months.

Fixers compare gold bangles
and straight men, baseball-capped, clap their hands
as a Tsarina in capri pants
sings the GI Blues,
while the blonde reporter with the tramp stamp,
who once bit a man's face in Baghdad
clutches her Tom Collins
and toasts to Io, the old cow,
who gave this strait its name.

Summoned, the water laps
and licks the boat's engines
with its whisky-coloured tongue,
dirtied by the city's leftover livestock
tipped out daily
from the backs of butchers' trucks.

At what current does water grow apprehensive?
A girl in a red bikini
stands upon the deck's edge
too scared to jump
through the thicket of flies.
She feels history bleeding into history.
She feels this boat party is just like the others —
no way of getting off.

Pushed, the girl shrieks in delight
as she pierces through the water
as the gladflies gather and the water whispers —
Io never shrieked.
What myth is this? The Bosphorus blurts
and shudders.
Waiting for the century,
or at least the day, to end.

HER FAULT

She reads a book and feels relieved.
The gloomy city suddenly makes sense.
It's the earthquakes.
Locals still live in trauma from the great one —
memories of tremors passed on to each generation,
like a wedding dress or varicose veins.

No longer feeling so estranged,
she nails down the furniture,
straps down the white goods,
buys a non-electric tin opener
and leaves a packed suitcase
by the door.

At night she listens out for the tectonic plates.
Not a 7 or a 9, of course,

but maybe a 3.2 would do.
A smallish tremor.
A book falling off its shelf, or an alarmed cat.
Something to write home about.

THE STRIP

A STORY BY ADAM THIRLWELL
WITH A POEM BY
ALEJANDRO ZAMBRA

1.

Tuesday

Today I started reading Alejandro's poem.

In London the light is grey and soft green and very sad.

I have decided to begin a journal.

Real work seems impossible. But what is real work? A novel, perhaps, a film.
A giant and coherent structure. All that seems possible now is the making
of very small notes.

Evening

In other words, lately I have been in a high dudgeon.

Thursday

This morning I read an essay by the painter David Salle on the paintings
of Laura Owens. I'd already enjoyed so much of what Salle said and so much
of what I'd seen of Owens's flat, improvised, multicoloured collage paintings,
but then I read this paragraph – and I found it so charming that the charm was
also overwhelming, the way a person must feel who's undergoing a religious
conversion:

> It has been terribly important to Owens that her paintings call attention
> not only to the conditions of their own making, but also to the social
> nexus in which they participate. The work of art is one link in a chain
> that includes gallerists, curators and critics, her fellow artists, and of
> course the viewer. This focus on the social system of art is, in part, the
> legacy of conceptual art as it has been filtered through the language
> of painting. Owen makes being a good citizen into an aesthetic.

This is exactly how I want to write, I thought! I want to make works that are
hospitable to the world – to let other things into a story, like for instance the
fact that I particularly read this essay because I'd been charmed by Salle's
essays from the moment his editor sent me a copy of his art writings – perhaps
because the editor simply thought I might be its ideal reader, and in a way
I was, given how much I liked it. But I wonder if it's possible for something

more than other people to be let in to a work, like maybe other people's forms as well – to become as other, or multiple, as possible.

It's as if my ideal work is something like a strip in Las Vegas or LA, a little series of constructions all hosted in one straight line: the Casino, Night Club, Restaurant, Drive-Thru... It's true that this morning I'm hungover but I'm also, I think, lucid. And in that case perhaps I can start with this poem I just began reading by Alejandro – and make something which includes this poem by my friend? Of course, since it's written in Spanish this is going to mean not just transcription but also translation, and I'm not sure my Spanish, my *chileno*, is as proficient as the poem's elegance deserves. But often, after all, if you want utopia you have to work for it – and certainly this is true of most major acts of friendship.

2 am

I always like to be utopian. It's my least unreliable mania. And perhaps there's something utopian in this wish to include in a work all the processes of its construction. It's why I felt such a sense of friendship when I read Alejandro's first novel *Bonsai*, with its little descriptions of its own making. Even if perhaps every attempt at total openness is always doomed to conceal things, and maybe it's even this hidden element which secretes the most vital truth.

Wednesday

The poem is by my friend Alejandro Zambra and is called 'Mudanza'. It's a long poem, in six sections, each about one or two pages. He sent it to me in an email and I printed it immediately, then kept it with me wherever I went without ever reading it. And now here it is. Even its title is a problem for translation. Mudanza! I understand its basic meaning, of movement, removal, one thing displaced to another location, but I can't exactly see how I'd translate this single word into another single English word. Also the poem's rhythm is very strange, with unexpected repetitions and line breaks, while the stories it's telling – of meetings, journeys, separations, some of which seem distinct, some of which seem related – remain enigmatic, as if something is being withheld.

It's as if it is by Alejandro and not by Alejandro, simultaneously: Alejandro before he became the Alejandro I first met.

Perhaps retrospectively you can recognise a persistent tenderness in his precision of language, like the care he takes at the ends of lines to split up and rearrange phrases; and certain images of shapes and sheets and anonymous miniature plants; and finally the delight he takes in repetition, his love of making and then breaking up a pattern. But this possible confusion and obscurity of identity don't, in the end, really matter because I can also recognise this poem's landscape very precisely. Alejandro wrote it when he was perhaps twenty-five or twenty-six. I know the apartment blocks and cigarettes he's describing, the bus terminals and train stations. The landscape of late youth! A series of transit decisions... Like the way I used to go in night-trains across Europe, from Madrid to Tangiers, or from Budapest to Prague. I was always very tired. I lived on sandwiches and cigarettes. And now I am thirty-nine, and Alejandro is forty-two.

Something has happened – between the writing of the poem and the writing of its translation – and one word for that, of course, is time. But there are other words.

I remember how when I was writing my first novel, when I was twenty-three, its potential publication was so distant as to be irrelevant, so I could write anything I liked – but then something is published, after all, and subsequently it becomes impossible not to be ever so slightly corrupted by the way all writing from then on will attain a public sheen. A certain sincerity and courage just become unavailable – or at least more difficult to achieve.

A List of Possible Translations for 'Mudanza'

Movement
In Movement
Removal
Transit
Time

Friday

Yesterday, I had to fly to LA for a meeting about a possible film.

On the plane I read Sei Shōnagon, partly because I remember that Alejandro loved it too, her *Pillow Book* – I think because of the way its elegance in no way understates her devastation.

'The attractiveness of a man depends largely on the elegance of his leave-taking.'

This morning I walked down Hollywood Boulevard, trying to orient myself on its strip of haphazard buildings. For some people, those who grew up here, the barbeque joints and roadhouses might be very boring, but to me they have golden allure. In this light, things move more slowly, or at least they seem to; perhaps they're simply more relaxed. In the window of a Thai nail salon was a shrine of carved wood and golden foil. A cat-god was enthroned, surrounded by three peaches and sachets of instant soup and incense sticks. A gold disposable lighter had been left behind among the peaches.

Then I came back to this hotel room. I felt very alone. Above me, there was a white ceiling fan, stilled. Behind me on the bed was a bag of shrimp crackers I had bought from a 24-hour store but then forgotten to eat – and the manuscript of this long poem by Alejandro.

Evening

Years ago, I slept with a girl in one of the cities mentioned by Alejandro. I liked her so much. She was much younger than I was: I was in my thirties, she was in her twenties. She came from Venezuela, and was a dissident in exile. She worked for a group who monitored freedom of speech. She kept a package of rolling tobacco in a miniature black plastic handbag that had an extravagant black fur plume. Why did you leave Caracas? I asked her. Because I was kidnapped, she replied.

I remember feeling ashamed, in some way, of how much I liked her, because if I were to introduce her to my friends they would not understand. They would only see someone so much younger, the boring exotic. They would think they understood the story. And of course, they would have been right. It was a fantasy, I understood this. (This is what I wanted to say to them.) But how else are you going to understand anything other than yourself, without some fantasy of metamorphosis?

Later

It's so lovely to be in this city, where the sun is always shining and every conversation is gently shadowed by money. The weather effects outside are spectacular: vast motionless skies, as if each building were a boat.

Saturday

I wonder if it's different, translating your friend, to translating someone dead, or at least translating someone you have never met? The responsibilities you feel as you consider each minute decision might be different, and therefore the decisions you make will be different too. With Alejandro, I feel at once very free, because he is my friend, and very constricted, because he is my friend. But then there are always responsibilities in every construction between two people. It's very complicated, the way you have to give equal attention to a person's multiplicities.

Maybe all translations should come with journals attached.

2.

Monday

The girl from Venezuela was called Soledad. The day after I met her, as I was on my way to the airport, she sent me a message. It said: *You got a girlfriend yet?* And while I realised that this was in some way meant to be funny, I also understood that it was surely packed with hidden meaning. I did not know how to reply in a way that was serious but also amused and complicit – the way it's always difficult to negotiate the hidden codes between two people. Perhaps all we really wanted was friendship, but it's very arduous, sometimes, to arrive at that state – the way you always have to learn how to read, every time you begin a new work. And this is only more complicated when sending messages to someone for whom your language is not their first language – you never know how much implication is intended in their messages or is only there by accident, an unintentional hazard of language.

Lunchtime

I'm writing this beside a swimming pool. A girl gets up from a lounger, tests the water with her hand. The rectangle of her phone is outlined in the back pocket of her jeans.

Evening

I spent this afternoon translating the poem's second section. I'm enjoying this change of identity so much – as if I could pull Alejandro's poem over me like a superhero's cape. It's a strange poem and I like this; it feels both improvised and highly organised, the way an unconscious might feel if you were ever to meet it in person. I haven't written poetry for a very long time, not since I was perhaps eighteen. I am fairly sure I will never write it again. So this will be the last poem I ever write, this poem translated from Chilean – just as it was the last poem my friend wrote before becoming a novelist.

Nothing Alejandro has published since this poem seems as private or obscured. And yet with this new section I'm feeling a kind of relief. It's more serene, more regular, even if my questions are only increasing. *Who is this woman who is travelling*? I want to ask him: *who is the speaker*? *How are these small stories related? Is the woman travelling the same person as the woman sleeping in the first section?* I was about to send him a message but then I thought: no. I don't want translation to be so *easy*. Also, whatever he might reply would still not satisfy me, I know this – it would only add another layer of possibility. For why, after all, should he be more of an authority than me? I understand the general atmosphere of the story being told – coffee and cigarettes in the elaborate soft dawn at bus terminals and subway stations. And in the end perhaps that's enough, to understand an atmosphere. It's like how when a friend is telling you a vast story which you can't quite follow – perhaps about their divorce or an illness in the family – all you can do is trust the voice in which they tell it. A voice is something that has the cunning to make itself heard for a certain time, and I wonder if one situation in which it might contrive such cunning is when it's trying to tell you a truth that is ever so slightly beyond it. You trust the sincerity of your friend's attempt to say something, or confide, even if what precisely she's confiding is a mystery. Just as I knew that this was the miniature book Alejandro wrote when he thought he would probably stop writing, but instead he wrote this poem that was unplanned, flowing, this poem which overtook him.

But still, it was probably the moments when this poem felt most private or mysterious which were making it difficult for me to joyfully maintain this experiment of existing in more than one language – like for example these people who *revuelven con los ojos la cerveza*. If I translate it literally, as people *stirring beer with their eyes*, I'm worried that people might doubt my *chileno* – because it's these changes in tone or deviations from ordinary speech which so often make people anxious about whether you truly do understand what's happening in another language. But at the same time I don't want to make the poem more ordinary than it is. Just as earlier I was troubled by the way to translate *pobremente – poorly dark*, I had written. Surely *poorly dark* was not a usual phrase – in either English or Spanish? And maybe this knowledge of what's usual and what's not is one way to measure true fluency – the other ways including, but not being limited to, the ability to swear, or use cliché, even if more and more

I wonder if in another language you should never use cliché, or little idioms like proverbs, since they will always have a suspect tone, the way it's suspect if someone speaks a foreign language with no accent at all. Maybe the only way to speak a foreign language is to speak an elegantly reduced version of it, to accept the modest limits of one's competence. Naturally in Spanish I have less vocabulary choice than someone who grew up in Santiago or Caracas. Which then creates the paradox that strangely, in any foreign language a person happens to speak, she might in fact express herself with more clarity than when using her first language, dependent as she is on reduced resources.

Dawn, jetlagged

This poem has the craziest tone. It keeps switching with each section. It's written in the vocabulary of administrative letters and real estate brochures, a kind of incantation. But also each section has its own particular concept, so that while that first section was a little studio of desolation, something which tried to maintain a rigour that was constantly being broken, the next section in fact managed to maintain its regularity – as if its presiding deity was fate. So that whereas at first I thought I would follow very closely the strange line breaks, this way of breaking up phrases in unlikely places, I'm now wondering if a true translation will in fact have to sometimes sadly choose more rhythm over wackier line breaks, even if that's also difficult to do.

Breakfast

The first time I wrote to Alejandro he replied two days later: 'Dear Adam: I read *Politics* two weeks ago. "You must read it," told me a friend who never fails. When I saw your name in the inbox I thought it was a joke... Thanks for that book, I enjoyed it a lot.' I liked this coincidence so much.

3.

Tuesday

Today I was waiting on the sidewalk for my Uber, looking at a row of sweet-gum trees, when a car went past me then pulled up at the curb. Inside were a man and a woman. The man got out and came up to me, asking for an address. He showed me his phone, with an email on it. It was from a lawyer, whose address was at the bottom of the message. *I'm not from here*, I tried to explain. *I have no idea where anything is.* His phone, I noticed, was set to a different time zone. It said the time was eight in the morning, when in fact it was three in the afternoon. It was a little disturbing. The engine was still running. I felt like I was failing them in a very dramatic moment of their lives. And we paused there, uncertain – until my car arrived and separated us forever.

I went to my meeting. A beautiful boy fixed me a coffee while I waited in a kind of antechamber. I felt very far from home. Hopelessly I remembered my parents. In our house my mother kept a terrarium, a large green bowl stoppered with a cork disc, inside which were ferns and mosses and small lianas. I suddenly missed this green miniature forest very much. And I was sorry that at some point in my history it had been removed or just destroyed and I had never noticed, even though my mother had tended to it with such beautiful care.

For some minutes I just sat there, stirring with my eyes the coffee.

Thursday

It's as if the voice I need will have to come up with its own system of repetition and variation – a system which isn't quite Alejandro's, or the poem's or my own, even if that kind of invention might require many moments of failure and depression. For instance, many phrases repeat themselves, but with minute alterations. A decision in this poem is rarely taken only once, and so I have to be sure that a phrase that worked in one location can also work in another – like the first words of the poem: *Me dijeron*. I could translate the phrase either as *They told me* or *I was told*, and since this phrase repeats itself many times it seems important to make an absolute decision on this. And so because in general I dislike all passive constructions, and am not sure of the status of this I – of any I, I guess – I think I will translate the phrase as *They told me*, although this then of course allows into the poem a *they* of whose identity I am not at all sure. But then maybe that's one of the pleasures of moving between languages, that it invents monsters and gremlins whose existence inside the poem is until this time not suspected at all?

Last night I flew back home.

I'd been thinking that I'd call the poem 'Removal', but now I wonder if perhaps 'Movement' is a better translation for 'Mudanza' than 'Removal'. Maybe the idea of removal is too limited to apartments and trucks – and perhaps Alejandro intended something more abstract. But I also like the ordinary sound of *removal*. At a certain abstraction, everything fails. The problem is that the word *mudanza*, like every word, has so many tendrils and sticky feelers connecting it to other words – like *muda*, meaning a change of clothes, or moulting or shedding leaves, but also *mute, silent, unspoken*; and then also concealing the dance of *danza* – but in another language those feelers and tendrils can never be the same. All you can do is produce a sketch and in the end therefore, I suppose, the anguish of translating the title is no different to choosing a title to a work more conventionally my own. As soon as something has a title then something else is lost; it clarifies but also reduces. And one thing I am having to learn is that reduction is not perhaps a tragic condition. Just as for instance some, perhaps much, of the repetition I am noticing in the poem is not important at all. While it might be sad that I can find no way of hinting that this word *grabar*, meaning *engrave*, for the initials in the book, sounds similar to the *grabadores*, the tape recorders, mentioned elsewhere in the poem, it's also perhaps something that the reader in Santiago would barely notice at all, and so its loss is, as so often, no disaster.

Midnight, jetlagged

A few years later, I saw Soledad again. I was back in her city. It was only the second time I had ever seen her, and yet I thought I knew her completely. We met in a diner. Everyone else there was old. I wondered if Soledad had chosen this place for our meeting because it was so exotic and at the same time unromantic. It emitted multiple signs and was therefore usefully ambiguous. When I walked in I couldn't immediately see Soledad, and so stood there, staring. There was a man on his phone, sitting in a booth. He stared back at me, pausing his conversation. I had a very conscious and uncomfortable sense of invading the intimacy of another person. Then finally I saw Soledad. In the booth beside us an older couple had finished two hamburgers. Both of them had left their two crinkle-cut slices of gherkin on the rim of the plate, and the napkin crumpled beside it. It was very touching, this symmetry of taste.

– Yeah but so I have this problem, said Soledad.
– Oh? I said.
– I have to look at two apartments now, she said. The agent called. And my boyfriend is away so I have to go see them.

I was relieved at the delicate way in which she mentioned she had a boyfriend, but also a little dejected at how my afternoon – which I'd imagined full of rare polyglot flirtation – had become so suddenly truncated. We walked outside and paused by a metal siding, painted with a landscape of palm trees and sea.

– You could come with me if you want, she said.

It was very difficult, judging the tone in which she said this sentence.

Friday

I should be writing this translation.

The first apartment we went to was in a part of town hidden between two freeways. Inside a store selling tinned corn and lentil soup there was a red Coke machine, which said in white writing: *Here's the Real Thing*. I had this feeling I often have when in a new city, of how much employment and industry there is in the world, and as always it impressed on me how little I understood about it. I would never know what it was like, to go shopping exhausted in the early evening after working all day at a machine plant, or an auto shop. I lived, instead, in a luxury of calm. And as so often I was amazed and also upset by the effects that money could impose on a world – the same way it had always meant for me that to travel was only ever an exercise in curiosity, in fantasy, never precarious or enforced or terrifying. Airports were always places of amusement and excitement and at the very worst just boredom. To move from space to space was never an achievement.

We were buzzed into a damp hallway. The agent met us at the apartment door. I felt just ever so slightly out of place, as if I were playing the part of the lover in an old farce. I went to try out kitchen cupboards, just opening and closing them; then I examined the boiler and its machinery. The bare light-bulbs and windows without blinds created a surprisingly savage or bleak effect. It had been a long time since I had rented an apartment, and that realisation made me feel old. Suddenly I was conscious of limits and impossibilities.

I wandered back into the living room where there was now another couple, also inspecting the apartment. I didn't know if I was meant to look in some way like Soledad's partner. For surely no one wanted the possibility of dark melodrama – to think that she was here with a man who was not her boyfriend? At the same time I did not want Soledad to think that I was acting excessively, or inappropriately.

– Is this your first place? a man asked me, in Spanish.
– Um, yeah, I said, in Spanish.

It seemed wrong not to allow this kind of illusion. Then Soledad came up to me.

– What do you think? she said.

She said this in English, loudly.

– I think we should see the other one, I replied.

Outside it was suddenly twilight, a kind of green darkness. In the trees, fireflies were zipping imaginary zips in the transparent air.

We went to a bodega for snacks but there was nothing we wanted: just rows and rows of packets – Japanese noodles and *sopas para uno*. We went to a burger joint and bought a package of fries and sat down on the sidewalk to eat. Soledad lit another cigarette. I looked up at the windshield of a car parked beside me. It was a mess of phone bills, coke bottles, pens, scissors, an old corn on the cob. It was so strange as to be delirious. She placed the package of fries between us on the ground, on top of some apartment brochures. Behind us was a barber. In the bright window, a man was sitting in his white shroud, wantonly hair-strewn, having the nape of his head dusted for clippings.

I felt something like happiness inhabit me. As if I were dissolved and at the same time still myself.

More Possible Titles

Las Vegas Strip
Honky Tonk
Journal of a Young Man

Sunday morning

'This stage in Argentinian civilisation, spanning between the years 1900 and 1930, presents curious phenomena. The children of shopkeepers study fantastical literature in the College of Philosophy and Letters; they are ashamed of their parents and in the morning tell off the maid if they find a discrepancy of a few cents in the bill from the market.' How much I love Roberto Arlt for this sentence!

Monday

What's currently slowing me down are the European place names in the poem's third section. I know that Alejandro once lived in Madrid, and I also remember that the final chapters of *Bonsai*, which he wrote after writing this poem, took place in Madrid. But I'm surprised to discover these other locations – like Bad Hersfeld, a spa town in Germany, or Elvas and Manresa, small historic towns in Portugal and Catalonia, and also Granada and its old districts: Albayzín and Sacromonte, where the Roma live. The virgin he mentions, I think, must be the patron saint of Granada, the Señora de Las Angustias, Our Lady of the Sorrows. This European detail is charming me but as the translator of this poem it also baffles me. I'm not entirely sure what it can mean – and therefore assume that its only meaning would be as facts in Alejandro's biography, quivering for him with private history – that they are places he was once in love, or saw a cat he adored. Maybe I'm wrong. Maybe he chose them at random. Or perhaps these references to Spain and its European surroundings are a way of measuring the distance between the language of this dying colonising power and the pristine contemporary *chileno* Alejandro speaks with such measured delicacy. For of course he is American. Naturally his idea of Europe will be different to mine. But presumably therefore I don't need to know their real meaning. Names after all can be evocative without ever being understood. Just as a poem, like a story or a voice, can move you without its mechanics ever being understood. The names are a problem for this poem's reader, not its translator.

Dawn

My parents' marriage recently broke down, and I am finding their emails to me unbearable. I do not know how to reply. *I am still a child!* I want to cry. *I am not an adult being!*

4.

Monday

At last, I feel like everything I do in English matches what I think the Spanish is doing.

Later

Mystery, like loss, is a category you acquire more and more. The word *reams*, for instance, occurring oddly on its own, worried me: *if and only if the / glasses, the scissors and the / reams, if and only if the sun might exit / prudently the scene...* Presumably it was obvious that it would mean *reams of paper* – for what other *reams* are there? – it was just, I had never seen *reams* used in this isolated way before, and I fleetingly wished that Alejandro had made this obvious.

It's as if the poem's entire meaning is elusive, a line of flight, as if its identity isn't in its meaning but in its movement – is this one way of putting it? – in the way it has of moving forward and then doubling back on itself, picking up phrases, reusing them, adding new words, a continuous process of repetition and variation. Maybe I should call it 'In Movement' because that's the sensation I'm experiencing – of being moved from one sentence or line to the next in a drifting motion which, even if it seems to obscure the sentences' meaning, is very pleasing. Just as I feel that there's a constant adjustment of distances in the poem which I'm finding very alluring, the way I enjoy in novels watching narrators move close to then further away from their characters. It's as if this idea of *movement* is a way of explaining everything.

Tuesday

But I haven't finished the story of the apartments.

The second apartment we went to was in a more elegant part of town. The apartment was in a new construction. Towers were arranged around a central courtyard. In the atrium, there was a small office for a dental practice. This apartment was larger, with a view of the city.

– I love this, I said.

Outside, there were lights everywhere: in offices, apartment blocks, small garages. I could imagine the way the light would come in, every morning, scattering shadows everywhere.

Soledad began asking about the possibility of furniture. Meanwhile, I went from room to room – a series of squares – and then I came back to the kitchen area, inside the living room. I leaned on the counter, looking out over the city. Soledad was still talking to the agent in the hallway, and I listened to her voice in the background. It felt incredibly strange, accompanying her on these visits. It felt more intimate than if we had slept together again, or at least that seemed a possible hypothesis. I felt happy and desolate, simultaneously. The city was a calm horizon, and I tried to imagine us sitting at this counter together, eating breakfast before she went to work in the morning; or how this room would hold our vast fiestas, narcotic and full of hope.

– So OK? said Soledad, coming back into the kitchen. You good? *Now* we can get a drink.

Thursday

What I like about the journal form is that it gives the illusion that each day is a process of thought. Everything is lost, of course, that's just the natural entropy of every day, but in a journal something might still be won from the basic defeat. Even a moment of reading – like this, from Ricardo Piglia's *Diario de Emilio Renzi*. 'The difficulty with not having much money is finding a place to be together. A room of one's own to make love. I'd have to write an essay on youth drifting through the city, begging for a place to lock themselves in.'

Later

Sitting here in a restaurant, the soft rainy greyness outside, waiting for my editor to arrive, I realise that the reason I don't like going out for lunch is that if it's too much of a cocoon then the rest of the day feels like a long disappointment.

A journal, like a translation, is a way of multiplying yourself.

5.

Saturday

There's something else I need to say.

The evening Soledad and I went apartment hunting, we'd already agreed that we would spend the night together. After we had visited the two apartments we stopped at her mother's apartment, where she was currently staying, so she could pick up some pills and a toothbrush. Then we went to my hotel and had dinner. We discussed what had happened between us. We had written many messages to each other, for many months, sincere and melodramatic, and there was a moment when I had promised that I would come and live with her. But of course, I had not. And so now we had a conversation in which she tried to understand what I had been thinking, when I wrote the kinds of things I wrote to her. She wanted to know at what point I had stopped believing in the possibility that we might be able to construct a new life together. Then we went up to my room. We explained to each other that we in no way needed to *have sex*, that this decision to spend the night together in the same bed only involved tenderness, nostalgia, affection. She went into the bathroom while I undressed and got into bed. Then she came back in, pulled back the duvet and exclaimed: *but you're naked!* There was delight in her voice but also, I now know, a tinge of regret.

She had acquired many tattoos since I had last seen her body.

The next morning we were lying there, and as I was thinking how much
I loved how she felt in my arms, so ensconced and elegant, she said, smiling:

– How did we end up in bed together? I never assumed this would happen.
I didn't meet you thinking that would happen.

I was surprised. I wanted to believe that she was lying, that of course she had
intended this ever since she had texted me saying she had taken the day off to
spend it with me. Because, I thought to myself, I had assumed it would happen.
Or at least, I had intended it as soon as I discovered she was going to be in the
city at the same time as me. Or if not intended, then I had thought about it as
something possible and fantastical.

But I didn't say this.

– Me neither, I replied.

But of course, we sometimes need better words than *intention*, to describe what
happens between two people. We had slept together, and now I wondered how
much she really wanted to, or more precisely how much the desire was total.
I remembered how the first time we slept together, many years ago, we went
up to a hotel room and she turned on the TV. *I don't want to watch TV*, I said.
We were lying on the bed. I thought it was obvious what we both wanted.
I kissed her. And she kissed me back.

Nothing is ever fully overt. Something is always withheld. It's like the way
a story cannot say what it has to say. It can only say it with the words it has,
which by definition are not precisely what it is saying.

6.

Sunday

This evening, on the TV, there was a football match. And it was beautiful,
just watching the miniature colourful people – and the camera panning from
right to left and back again. Then I stopped watching and looked up a video
of Alejandro on YouTube, where Alejandro, so much younger, is reading part
of his poem – outdoors, at a festival perhaps, somewhere in Latin America. It
seemed to have been recorded on someone's phone. In the audience there was
a baby sleeping in its father's arms.

Evening

After seeing Soledad for the second and perhaps last time, I was in the transit airport somewhere – in America or Europe, São Paulo or Paris, I can't remember – when I received an email she had written to me as I flew over the ocean. She said that she wanted to explain something to me that she had not been able to explain in conversation. She wanted to say that something had now changed in her life. She had been very depressed, for some time, but now things were different. In the years we had not seen each other, I had represented something pure to her, something untouched by life. I was a fantasy, she wrote, but now it was time to give up this kind of fantasy. We should of course remain friends, she added, but we should stop inventing futures based on something that was not real.

It was a very poised note, sometimes in Spanish, sometimes in English. In the most gentle way possible, she explained that she was angry with me, without ever saying that she was angry. She explained, without ever exactly saying this, that I had stopped being a fantasy, and had become simply another man. I had bored her with desire. It was an elegant and lethal leavetaking, and it was as if I could love her even more, precisely as she explained that we had never known each other, and said goodbye.

I shut my computer, and sat there looking out at the various planes.

Still evening

It's kind of incredible, the damage time does to a person – I mean the habit it has of reducing your life to a single point. The more I feel this sensation, the more the past seems to emerge everywhere. In the poem's final section, I saw, there was a mention of Malasaña, a district I remember in Madrid with little bars and cafés, and I imagined that this district was where Alejandro lived, when he lived in Madrid. When I was eighteen I had once got very drunk there, and slept most of the next day in a park. I woke at twilight to find that someone had stolen my bag, in which was a postcard I had been meaning to send to my parents.

Our youth was over, and that included a certain precarious but joyful way of living. It was a tender feeling that was now inhabiting me, and I hoped that perhaps tenderness would be one feeling that would emerge if I managed our construction right, I mean this work or strip in which I would include my transcription of his poem, as well as the circumstances and anxieties that had occurred in the process of its translation. It's like when you look at a city and have to admit you love all its curlicues and mismatched styles – its honky tonk decoration. They are, as the saying goes, what we have. This was the construction I aspired to – the way a friendship can continually include each other's pasts and futures and not be broken. I wanted to make a whole that included as much as possible, or at least seemed to, otherwise why bother with this kind of work – the imaginary repetition of real experiences? Naturally it would be full of gaps, with imperfections and pieces missing, but I hoped that this would not prevent it being a world – the way Sei Shōnagon created the Emperor's court 1,000 years ago in Japan, just through her lists and observations. And maybe in fact it would be precisely because there are such gaps and pieces missing that a construction can form a world. Perhaps that's what we mean, when we call something a world.

Night

Just now I almost called my mother but remembered that it was the middle of the night. Instead I'll call Alejandro in Mexico City, as he sips the evening's first mescal, and ask him what he's doing.

MOVE
Alejandro Zambra

1.

They told me to inform them thirty days
in advance they told me to inform them
thirty times at least they told me to at
least inform them thirty times and that
in times like these you shouldn't –
you couldn't – work. That I should leave,
go two blocks down and ask
if there might still be soup for one a
half bottle for one they told me it was
half possible there might be a bottle
and they were right:
                                    if you like it you like it
if you don't you don't, that's all
they told me they were right and they were right:
the girl is weak and white and you are
poorly dark that's all there is
not in but on the surface of the bed
when you kiss and are kissed.
                                    It gets dark, while falls
not night but something and between the sheets
a dangerous form which moves
like a shape from which you try to escape.
Or you stay, they told me, and decide to fall –
like night – prostrate at the feet of the
feet of the lover who sleeps without knowing
you are sleeping beside her. And how painful the
bright darkness in the arms at the base of the night.
                                    Or below,
arranged from left to right, thirty nights
with their days between the sheets
which watch over and enclose us and
watch over us, packed up in boxes
which they open many times
with their days and their nights with their times
and their days, until they just in case
change all the locks just in case
you do come back it doesn't matter

if the key falls out of your pocket
nor do you have to scrape out
all the gunk from the mouldy cup. Don't refuse
to wave at us, don't refuse our money
we have no more cigarettes
because in nights
like these you can't – you mustn't –
work, you can't – you couldn't –
do favours nor attend to the voices
which tell you: she sleeps at night
beside you and doesn't know because she is sleeping,
she kisses and you kiss her, that's all
there was not in but on the surface
of the bed packed for thirty days,
thirty times they informed me to tell them
I was leaving and would never come back. Don't
refuse our cigarettes, that I should go very calm
if you like it and shut my mouth if you don't,
it doesn't cost you anything to do us the favour
of sitting so prudently waiting for news
so very calm so very seated while falls
not night but something and a
dangerous form shifts in your memory
like a shape from which you try to escape.

2.

She travels long hours and doesn't arrive at her destination,
there are signs with her name, people
waiting for consignments and she travels long
hours and doesn't arrive and that's all: it was the hand,
it wasn't me who was waving, it was the shadow
it wasn't me who hid on the innermost platforms
and urgently asked them to turn down
the volume: she travels long hours, there are
signs with her name, they turned down the
volume to a buzz, a hum, many times
the planes or the buses pause for a moment
and refuel as meanwhile
they eat snacks or talk special effects
and their gloved hands get warmer.
They turn down the sound of the engines

but they come as soon as the people
glancing at newspaper columns are saying
or discussing or stirring with their eyes
a beer. She travels long hours
and doesn't arrive. She sleeps as they cross
the border, she never knew they were serving
her breakfast that right now they'll encounter
turbulence, it wasn't me who waved
attentively who asked them
to fill up the tank until it overflowed
because in days like these you can't –
you mustn't – make promises in the air
it's not right to examine the thick gunk
of the coffee nor engrave one's initials
on a book that much later
dissolves in your memory; or on whiteboards
with marker pens which exasperate the signs
which are deleted when they say she
didn't come, that she's still sleeping without knowing
that they experienced turbulence, she travels
so peacefully without reaching her destination,
there are people waiting with signs
and with whiteboards, it wasn't me
who waved at her carefully with
the perfectly dyed eyebrows
of people who discuss principal scenes
while waiting for their consignment's arrival –
the suitcases, the marker pens, the hums,
the signs, the destination and the beers.

3.

They took the words out of my mouth,
the five or six lines I would say
if they suddenly came back with the change
and the chairs reupholstered:
tape recorders that repeat various voices
so sure that someone is listening.
The telephone calls fail,
it's very late in Madrid and in Bad Hersfeld
it's very late in Elvas and in Manresa,
in Granada they took the cigarettes

out of our mouths
and in flight we reached
the lookout. Someone said that the virgin
might not be delayed, someone said we might wait
for the dealer, might engrave our names
just once, that we might collect the money
in the mean time.
Night falls over Quito
and in Santiago
thirty radio announcers extend the angles
of a problem with multiple
angles: tape recorders which repeat
various voices so sure that someone is
listening. She travels long hours to Granada,
she hopes that the virgin may not be late,
dawn arrives in Albayzín and the drinkers
we feel that this time
was different, that the nails rusted over
and the silence
was a kind of suppressed gasp,
that the virgin doesn't improve with the years.
Dawn arrives in Sacromonte and in Santiago
and in Bad Hersfeld the clocks go forward.
Today is the longest day,
tonight is the longest night –
they warn us that tomorrow's newspapers
won't cover the news, that it's cold,
that we should close our windows
and eyes
                         because in days like these
you can't – you couldn't – do favours
nor pay attention to the things which tell you
the cards of destiny:
                              to the jail
but quickly, the water works the hospital new york
avenue but quickly, she is weak
you are white but only sometimes,
each time what you don't know
begins again, don't refuse
to wave at us, we have no more
cigarettes, it no longer matters that you wake up
when you wander in the night nor that you lose
the game or the cut so many times

fate is foretold and the mouth's form
alters when you drink:
telephone calls fail
it's very late in Bad Hersfeld and in Madrid
it's very late in Elvas and in Manresa
in Granada they take the cigarettes
out of our mouths and we arrive at the lookout,
we were searching for a place when we saw you
and wanted to know if it ever upsets you
that we could pass distantly through the night,
so many times fate is foretold, telephone calls
fail; they took the words out of
my mouth, these four or five lines I would say
if they suddenly came back with the change
and the chairs reupholstered.

4.

(It was the hand
it wasn't me
who was waving:
once upon a time there was a hand
a single hand
a hand and an arm
once upon a time there was an arm
searching blindly
in the bottom of
a bag.

And so the bag and the arm –
and the hand –
came to a
compromise.
They came to this, a compromise:
the arm could stay
with the hand and the bag
could stay
with the hand and the arm
if and only if
the glasses, the scissors and the
reams, if and only if the sun might exit
prudently the scene

if and only if the cigarettes
might maintain a strict silence
if the discreet coffee might pool
and the eyes above all
the eyes might limit themselves
to observing
the plants which grow
stoic anonymously
while falls
not night but
something: a dangerous shadow
that covers at once
the latches
the corridors and the writer
who stirs and re-stirs his beer –
he does that,
stirs and re-stirs his beer,
waves to the camera
says something, a noise, in order to say something
makes forms with his hand
and with his eyebrows
with his arm gets
the papers revises
the lines he has to say
and decides for example
to clean the bathroom tiles
to revise his unsent
messages, to begin
from now in
lower-case:

the arm can stay
with the hand and the bag
can stay
with the hand and the arm
but the hand always ends up alone
carefully alone
poor hand alone
that therefore waves
carefully to the person who.)

5.

Every now and then it begins again, an improvised
sentence: a short rest on the stairs
doesn't permit too many niceties
and the signs are lost when you pass by
with your arms encumbered. Half
tones or sour aftertastes, scars at the mouth,
we missed them – barely – the nuances
that now overflow when I search
with patience, frame by frame,
lines in the face, half tones and
sour aftertastes: someone poses
uncertain of her own face,
someone removes with suspicion and energy –
with their hands, with their eyes – the
fragments of accumulated sand,
frame by frame the horizon gets dark,
someone travels long hours seated
at the back and doesn't know how much
is still missing, she is young and white, you are
weakly dark and that's all
there was not in but on the surface of the bed
when you kiss and are kissed; and so we kept,
therefore, the adjustments to the skirt,
we held them, like that, with needles, the façade,
the hems, the insignia, the insects
as they scale a lapel, the continuous horizon
dawns and she laughs or despairs, she weeps
or recovers the truth, she waits for them
to understand that love is a form
of incident, an adjustment of noise
in the image, some days, some nights
with their voices and their voices and their pauses:
we decided the times, we reviewed
the pauses, we overheard the voices
and a dangerous form chose for us
the road, a rest on the stairs doesn't
permit too many niceties, she sleeps
without knowing that they will encounter
turbulence, someone covers the half tone with
two hands
of painting, every now and then it begins again

what you now don't know and the signs
are lost when you pass by with your arms encumbered.

6.

While falls not night but something
greyish emerges: an underground shoot,
an abdominal effort, the prose
this morning doesn't feature
extensive digressions, instead now I encounter
soundlessly
the thresholds, the inner
corridors, the latches, the rests
and pauses. Now I water my garden
100% hoping for infectious
shoots to thrive when so many others
might jam the locks in case
someone changes the initials, leaves
our fiestas and forgets his script,
it's now that finally begins
the procession of faces which never acted,
never said their lines
nor left their coats in the cloakroom
and that's why now I invent
with its features other pauses other
distended voices that discuss in
silence that ask what's therefore
the idea: to pack up the instruments
is the idea, that they should keep the seats
if they want to, they just informed me
that I should tell them when I went, it wasn't me
waving carefully, where I'm leaving
the scissors for now, that they should keep
the cigarettes and clothes I don't expect
fair prices or convincing signs
because in days like these you can't
– you couldn't – do favours nor consider
the voices that tell you: she sleeps
through the commercials, already they're reading
the poems you prepared, this day
is the longest day, this night the longest night,
that the silence may therefore be a useful excuse

while we put the clocks back
and hope flickers while taxis
and buses pass by: that the complaints, the pastiches,
the latches, the thresholds, these pauses
I thought of offering remain outside:
they told me to inform them thirty days
in advance, they told me to inform them thirty
times at least, we decided
the times, we reviewed
the pauses, we overheard
the voices and a dangerous form
chose for us the road, a dangerous form
dissolves in your memory like
a shape from which you try to escape
while falls in Malasaña
not night but something
and the whores and the junkies were left with
the change: that they should keep the crib
and magazines, that they should
accommodate as they can this shape in the road,
review with care their sins and bills,
they're just missing the floor-tiles desserts and signatures,
every time moods synchronise and she forgets
that she travels long hours and doesn't arrive and
that's all: a short rest on the stairs doesn't permit
too many precisions and the signs
are lost when you pass by
with your arms encumbered, they took
the words out of my mouth, these four or five
times with their voices and pauses
I thought of offering: they lower the volume
to a buzz, a hum, it was the hand it wasn't me
who was waving, they told me to inform them
thirty days in advance, thirty
times they informed me
I should leave and never come back.

Santiago de Chile, mayo de 2003
London, April 2018

MARY RUEFLE   INTERVIEW

The first contact I had with Mary Ruefle was through her website. Against a black landing page, five headings in yellow serif font float, suspended in HTML darkness. Clicking on the 'contact' link redirected me to a cruel joke: 'Surprise! I do not actually own a computer. The only way to contact me is by contacting my press, Wave Books, or by running into someone I know personally on the street.' This message hovered next to an image of an empty stone font resembling a bird bath, over whose basin had been taped the words 'The Unknown'.

Since Ruefle lives in Bennington, Vermont, a chance encounter seemed unlikely. Instead, I got in touch with her 'people'. Doing so marked the beginning of a generous correspondence unfolding over several months, all via 'snail mail'. A reflection of her devotion to the materiality of writing, Ruefle writes almost exclusively by hand, a habit which does nothing to inhibit her productivity. She has published eleven books of poetry, two volumes of prose and one comic, alongside a collection of lectures. She has also made some ninety-nine erasure books, a ritual to which she dedicates herself daily. I was reminded of this each time she returned the transcript of our interview, cross-hatched with red ink, and little white shadows of Tippex.

'Wite-Out' forms a kind of scar, evidence of one formulation of thought deleted at another's expense; it is also a gesture of illumination, of 'burying and bringing to light'. Ruefle's writing pinpoints little snags in the fabric of the ordinary – a woman suddenly too fearful of the light inside her refrigerator to access a pitcher of water, or that 'feeling of frightening abundance' that descends when you realise there is altogether 'too much shampoo and too much toothpaste, too much pollution, dirt, rocks and grass' in this world. Rote gestures, like sweeping crumbs from the kitchen counter, gain dimensions of tenderness wilfully repressed in everyday life. As Ruefle confesses: 'I like to turn ordinary actions into *an encounter*'.

A preoccupation with dust, dishcloths and petroleum jelly is a political preoccupation, with the fibres that constitute a life. Rather than offering a self-conscious lesson in the personal-as-political, Ruefle reconstitutes the banal as a site of mystery and intrigue. This childlike inquisitiveness trails her work, irrespective of scale; it sticks as readily to blockbuster questions (about sex, death, even poetry itself!) as to small-fry.

In one letter, Ruefle asked if I'd seen *Lady Bird*, praising it as a 'fine film'. When Lady Bird expresses tearful, morning-after disappointment that her first sexual experience wasn't all she'd imagined, her irritating boyfriend, Kyle, is disdainful. Her pain, he assures her, ranks low on a hierarchy of suffering compared with that, say, of Iraqi civilians murdered by the US military. Lady Bird retorts sharply: 'Different things can be sad.' The line's comedy relies on an adolescent brand of narcissism that risks being totally charmless. But it endears Lady Bird to us precisely because it conceals the gnarly fact that suffering is nuanced, that it can't always be scaled-up to have global significance. The sufferings of the world can feel gargantuan; still, that doesn't lessen the sting of that 'orange sadness' of 'things left overnight in the oven and forgotten'. During our correspondence, Ruefle exhorted me to 'think about the lost moments in [my] own life'. I hope this interview prompts readers to do the same.   CECILIA TRICKER

TWR   When did you first begin writing poetry? Can you remember the first poem you wrote?

MR   I think I was around eight, I don't remember exactly, but by the age of ten I was reading and writing poetry not only in school on assignment but out of school, alone at home in my room. To me, the more interesting question is this: at what age does a child have their first experience of making a metaphor? Mine, as I have narrated elsewhere, happened at eight, when I looked at cracked bare earth and thought of it as a map – every chunk of dry dirt looked like a separate country being charted, and I was stunned by this fact, for I knew I was looking at dirt, but I was seeing a map.

TWR   First poem and first metaphor – that's two very formative experiences in one year. You've said elsewhere (in a 2014 interview with *Brooklyn Rail*) that you often describe yourself as being 'eight years old at heart'. Do you still experience the same sense of wonder when making metaphors? Do they still creep up on you in the same way they did at that age? (One metaphor of yours I particularly love is in 'Müller and Me', where 'the cemetery looks made of books and the library is a graveyard').

MR   No, making metaphors doesn't create a sense of wonder, what creates a sense of wonder is the human brain, in which metaphors arise spontaneously and unexpectedly (as they don't 'exist' in nature); for me, it's the brain behind the act that now astonishes me, the mysteriousness of our brains, and, of course, life itself in all its forms, plant, mineral, and animal. But yes, metaphors still 'creep up', there's no other way, they are sudden things. As for the metaphor you mention: well, a library *is* a graveyard – most of the authors are dead – and a graveyard *is* a library, each person buried there has a story.

TWR   You've mentioned that you had a military childhood, during which I imagine you moved around a lot, attending schools in Europe as well as in America. Was writing a constant for you during this time? Did this experience of travelling around, or being uprooted, shape your early writing?

MR   Writing has been a constant for as long as I can remember. The experience of moving around simply means I have no roots the way others might, I only saw my grandparents and cousins every three or four years, that kind of thing, and I don't write many poems that are centred on the family;

I have friends who have very large, close-knit families and it always amazes me, I can't imagine what that would be like, despite the fact that I have a formidable imagination.

TWR   Is place an important aspect of your writing? Where do you tend to write?

MR   Place isn't important, I tend to write in my head, which I can carry with me wherever I go.

TWR   You've been publishing poems for over thirty years, but your first collection of prose (*The Most of It*) was only published in 2008. Was there a particular catalyst for this shift from one form to another? Or were you always writing prose during this time?

MR   I was always writing prose; all my early books of poems have a prose piece in them, and then one day I had a very good editor who suggested a particular piece of prose be edited out of a book of poems on the grounds it was prose. From that moment on I kept my prose in a separate folder. The prose pieces in *The Most of It* span thirty years, because I'd been saving them; the ones in *My Private Property* were all written after *The Most of It*, and so span eight years. For a long time I wasn't writing prose except in an extremely intermittent way, and now it is a constant. Which might explain those numbers.

TWR   How does the experience, or process, of writing one, differ from the other?

MR   I am asked this question many times; the process is different insofar as my poems begin in my head with a loop of language that is already lineated (or feels that way) and the prose begins with an experience or subject I want to write about. I may not know how I feel about this subject or how I want to write about the experience, but the prose is pre-grounded in ways my poems aren't. So they begin differently, but the actual experience of writing – the exhilaration, the suspension of time – is identical in both cases.

TWR   When you say a 'loop of language', I am reminded of an earworm. In the introduction to *Madness, Rack, and Honey*, you describe poetry as 'a wandering little drift of unidentified sound' – to pin it down is like 'following the sound of a thrush into the woods' (the same line also appears in 'Greetings My Dear Ghost'). Almost like something that is overheard, a kind of eavesdropping.

MR   Yes, the poems are more elusive, they *are* like earworms, wandering, unidentified things I try to follow with my ear, while the prose is more like a brainworm, a squiggling thought I try to stretch out and examine.

TWR   How do you go about building your essays – the lectures collected in *Madness, Rack, and Honey*? Formally speaking, they don't always feel entirely distinct from your prose or your poetry.
MR   I pick a subject and I say everything I can think of to say about it – everything that interests me, that is. I don't like writing lectures, talks, that kind of thing, and yet that's what people want, they would rather listen to a talk than hear a reader. Why is that? What makes me sad makes other people happy. Magazines will solicit work from me and when I send a poem they will say 'Oh, we were hoping for a talk'. This summer I was in a book-store and the number of shelves devoted to writing *about* poetry was greater than the number of shelves devoted to poems themselves. I stood there staring at these shelves, it was proof of something, and it dismayed me.

TWR   I wanted to ask you something about craft, or perhaps more specifically about the material act of writing, and its relationship to technology. You don't have a computer (a seeming impossibility in the modern world!), and you've said elsewhere that you still write by hand, or a combination of hand- and typewriting. How does this affect the process of your writing? (I find that my thoughts often move too quickly on a com-puter, that I type before I have actually completed a thought. Writing by hand feels somehow more laboured, or considered to me.)
MR   I write by hand because that is how I began, and I love it. Moving the wrist, the marks the pencil or pen leave on the paper – like the trail of a snail – well, it is like drawing, no, it *is* drawing, and I am so enamoured of this activity that sometimes I write continuously without actually forming real words, I call it 'fake handwriting', and it's just as much fun as actually 'writing'. By fun I mean it's just as much a mystery. This whole wrist-moving action is why I write in the first place. I don't like tennis, or knitting, I like writing with my hands.

TWR   I'm reminded of the Surrealists and the practice of automatism in drawing and writing. Is any of this 'fake handwriting' ever usable, does

it make it into your work? Or is it just a reflexive exercise or a form of procrastination? I'm reminded also of 'If All The World Were Paper', where the speaker claims that they are 'only pretending to write' in much the same way the reader is 'only pretending to read', since both are imaginative acts.
MR   None of the fake handwriting ever makes it into a piece of writing, but some of it looks nice framed and hung on the wall. No, it's not procras-tination, nor is it an exercise, it's an activity. I don't do it very often. But there are writers, like Renee Gladman, who have become artists (visual artists) through thinking of writing as drawing.

TWR   How does writing by hand affect your relationship to deletion, or correction? Thanks to technology most writers can easily redact their work – does the absence of a delete key impact your own editorial process?
MR   I don't understand why someone would think writing by hand would make correction difficult – you just cross things out! And remember, pencils come equipped with erasers on their ends. I wonder if it has ever occurred to your generation that *Middlemarch* was written entirely by hand!

TWR   You have also published one book of 'erasure poems', *A Little White Shadow* (2006), made by 'disappearing' text from a nineteenth-century novella using white-out. You've made forty-five (perhaps more now!) one-off erasure books, some of which have been displayed in galleries, or published in journals. In your essay 'On Erasure', you describe the process as like 'writing with your eyes instead of your hands'. Can you tell me more about that? What do you like so much about the erasure form?
MR   I've made ninety-nine erasure books! Making them is a daily practice, I work on one first thing in the morning. It's meditative – the whiting-out process can be like painting a wall – but finding the text within the text can be invigor-ating, or alternately frustrating when I can't find anything to work with. When that happens I'll skip that page and return to it another day and see possibilities I didn't see before, which happens with poems too, and other forms of art-making; when you return to something you see it with another pair of eyes.

TWR   Can we also think of invisibility in nega-tive terms? In your piece 'A Half-Sketched Head', the speaker describes meeting a French feminist who asks her: 'How can women describe their feelings in a language that was primarily devised by men to describe theirs?' In the same piece, you also imagine 'the number of poems thrown away by the women who wrote them'. This seems to me a very sad, rather than joyous kind of invisibility – a lost canon of women writers.

MR   No, no, that was not a French feminist (though presumed at first) that was THOMAS HARDY: a direct quote! I love Thomas Hardy. Great female characters. But to answer your question, yes, invisibility can be, and most often is, negative: the plight of the invisible victim, in all circumstances, is a travesty. Women, people of a different race, or orientation, who have been for so long 'overlooked', ignored: that is the sadness of invisibility. At the same time, all lives, with a few exceptions, are invisible, overlooked, ignored: that is a fact of life. And one day all of Shakespeare will be destroyed, so it is a fact of life on this planet for *everyone*, even the so-called 'immortal'. But still, to have lived, to have been alive, there is no substitute for that. Think of Anne Frank at a birthday party... her excitement, her little dress. Lost canons! Think about the lost moments in your own life.

TWR   A lot of your writing (I'm thinking in particular here of *My Private Property*) seems to enact a kind of de-familiarisation. You are very attentive to objects or processes we might typically consider 'banal', or otherwise take for granted. One example that comes to mind is in 'The Invasive Thing', where the automatic gesture of brushing crumbs from a countertop acquires an existential, almost spiritual resonance. Similarly in 'Observations on the Ground', where the idea of planting a seed is reframed as a form of burial (this had never occurred to me before, and I found it so wonderful!). Do you feel yourself drawn to 'the ordinary' or 'the normal' when you're writing?

MR   I live an ordinary, banal life, so I am of course drawn to everyday activities, like brushing crumbs off the counter or peeling an orange. At the same time I have a racy imagination, and I like to think about things, so I think it's a matter of these two colliding. I like to turn ordinary actions into *an encounter*. It may sound strange, but in this way I love life.

TWR   You're very good at explaining things, despite what some of your titles would have us think ('The Woman Who Couldn't Describe a Thing If She Could'). At times I felt like the book could be utilised as an instruction manual for an alien species encountering humanity for the first time.

MR   Well, what if, every day, we woke up and behaved as if we were encountering life for the first time – wouldn't making breakfast become an interesting thing, wouldn't getting dressed be strange and amazing? Perhaps people who are bored by their routines and rituals should play this game, it might help them to love their lives a bit more ardently.

TWR   I think that would be a very restorative game. In 'Impersonal Problems' you write: 'Sometimes I think I am of a species that is bored to extinction, or that I am the last of such a species whose predominant trait was boredom.' In a 2015 *New York Times* piece Rivka Galchen described boredom as 'a failure of perception': 'We can never legitimately be bored by the world... There is no boredom out there. There is only boredom in here, in the mind.' How do you see boredom? Is it a failing?

MR   I agree with Rivka Galchen, but at the same time boredom is a *huge* subject, and many different things can be said of it. I am not bored by a situation that bores most people: being alone with nothing to do. But I *am* bored by certain situations that do not seem to bore some others: being at a party with more than eight people, standing in a room where you mingle and chat in snatches – nothing bores me more. Art openings. And certain books, certain films; I am sure Rivka Galchen is bored by certain books and certain films. So in this sense boredom is also a subject of class, of politics, and of individual sensibility. Think about what bores you, and how that might define you; think of what bores other people and how that might define them. Plenty of people think poetry is boring, and I have to admit there are *days* I agree with them, and I could be happy if I never read or wrote another poem as long as I lived. (I don't feel this way about prose, which is curious to me.) The rich must get bored by their own glitz, and the poor in my town are very bored by their lives, I can see that, there is very little possibility for them and they sit on their porches drinking beer, fanning their faces with gossip magazines... So you see, boredom, what constitutes boredom, is a huge subject. A middle-class life is mainly one of routine, repetitive responsibilities and all of that (at least for me, I live one) and it can be boring; as John Berryman said, 'Life, friends, is boring... Ever to confess you're bored means you have no Inner Resources.' *Reading* bores many people; I know someone who thinks history is boring! If you look down on these people, what does that say about you, and your sense of superiority? My sister once said to me that she thought intellectuals were boring because they never *did* anything, and by that she meant they were not active people, they spent too much time reading, they never got out and enjoyed life. An active life versus a contemplative life has long been a subject unto itself.... I don't mean to get carried away, I just want to say that I think boredom is a very interesting subject with ramifications you wouldn't expect at first. I am reminded, too, of a radio interview I once heard with a Holocaust survivor, where she said there was no greater gift than an ordinary, boring day.

TWR   Do you have any writing rituals?
MR   Except for my daily erasure work I have none. But I'm not done thinking about boredom; I want to say that the things that bore us can change as we grow and age. For instance, when one is young there is a great deal of melodrama involved in finding a partner, or in figuring out what you want to do with your life and where you want to live, how you want to live and all of that. We engage in many activities that will later bore us. Haven't you heard older parents sigh and say that the problems of their children are tiresome? But when children are young, their problems are never tiresome to their parents! So over time you have a shifting in what bores you; when I was young I thought many adults were perfectly boring because they just sat around their homes, presumably doing nothing, and now that is exactly what I like doing most of all! Boredom can change, the kind of music you listen to can change, the kind of clothes you wear, and all of that. Boredom is a river of change, like everything else.

TWR   In 'On Secrets' you suggest that writing requires some degree of invisibility, that 'poems are written in secret'. What do you mean? Is writing an inherently private practice?
MR   I think writing a lyric poem is an inherently private practice. At least for me it is, because I never envision an audience when I am writing a poem, but when writing an essay I always envision an audience – I wouldn't be writing an essay in the first place if it were otherwise – and though I've never written a novel, I think it would be madness to write one without a reader in mind. But poems? I think more poems get written than are ever read, poems are such urgent brief things, like laughing or crying; they happen, and then they vanish. Letter-writing interests me most of all; it is private yes, but it is also public insofar as it is meant to be read by another. Letter-writing is my favourite genre, next to haiku. If I could write only letters and haiku for the rest of my life, I would feel my writing had not been in vain. But keep in mind letter-writing and haiku bore most people nowadays! Oh boredom, the never-ending subject.

TWR   You seem concerned also with the small, and the shrunken – 'little golf pencils', 'little keys', dolls, empty matchboxes made to look 'like tiny presents' in a Christmas display. There is a scene in the title poem of *My Private Property*, where you describe a young girl 'communing' with a shrunken head (with which she has fallen in love). I feel like this is a gesture of your poetry, the act of 'communing' with the inanimate. (Also – I had never thought about wallet-sized photographs as shrunken heads!) Where does this interest in the miniature arise from?
MR   I do love the miniaturised, but I am not alone in this fetish. Take dolls. No, I don't have a collection of dolls or anything, but given the choice between going to an art museum or a doll museum I would probably go with the dolls. A more sophisticated person might want to look at the earliest clay figure of a human being found in the British Isles (I've seen a photograph) but what's the difference, who's to say if the figure may have been made by a father or mother to give to their child as a doll? And remember, dolls have dolls! It is a long hall of mirrors we make of ourselves. It is impossible to talk about without writing a book, but to animate an inanimate figure is an act of poetry every child has experienced. If you take a stick and draw a face on it you've made a doll; I'm not only speaking of manufactured dolls. The psychology of dolls fascinates me; child psychologists will watch their clients playing, playing they can enact feelings they might not be able to articulate in words. But when the doll talks back to you! That is the great moment. This is such a huge subject I can't go on. We would have to talk about boys playing with guns and all of that. I read once of an experiment

where boys dismembered the dolls they were given, and girls coddled and sang lullabies to the trucks they were given – what are we to make of that?

TWR   I suppose we'd also have to get into the whole bizarre fact of social conditioning, and how culture shapes these kinds of 'play' along gendered lines. I think I read something recently about people in the US naming their guns, and about babies being named after guns...
MR   Nothing that happens in the United States surprises me! Isn't that sad? Babies being named after guns! Is that an act of imagination or a sick, horrid thing? The imagination can be sick and horrid...

TWR   I just looked up the dismembering experiment but was led instead to 'the Bobo Doll Experiment', which was used to study aggression in children during a series of experiments in the 1960s. I used to swap my dolls' heads with the removable heads of plastic dinosaurs as a child. Did your dolls ever talk back to you? What did they say?
MR   I am certain my dolls talked back to me, but I don't remember what they said. I imagine they either comforted me or admonished me, depending on the situation we found ourselves in, whether I was feeling victimised or guilty.

TWR   Does your interest in the diminutive, and dolls in particular, also have something to do with the uncanny process of differentiating between the ersatz and the 'real'? I'm thinking here of the speaker's confusion in 'Recollections of my Christmas Tree' at how the matchboxes in her mother's ceramic Christmas display will remain empty, how they won't also contain fake presents. It's just *pretend*, rather than *real pretend*.
MR   The difference between *pretend* and *real pretend* is going the extra mile: you can pretend to feed your doll by raising a spoon to its mouth, or you can go the extra mile and put porridge in the spoon and wipe it off her lips.

TWR   So you believe we can have 'real' interactions, 'real' communications, even with inanimate figures or objects?
MR   Yes, I believe we can have real interactions with our imagination, interactions in which the inanimate is fully brought to life, and if it were not so, how could children do it every day, how could shamans do it century after century? Are children and shamans beneath consideration, are they contemptible? Are shamans children who never grew up? Are they stupid?

TWR   It feels like we encounter children – in particular, young girls – in quite a lot of your poems. Are any of these versions of your child-self? What kind of child were you?
MR   I never noticed that there were a lot of children in my poems, and I can't say if any of these are versions of my child-self, I'd have to look at the poems you are referring to. I don't think about my work in any of the ways a reader might – I think about the work of the authors I read, and I don't 'read' myself. What kind of child was I? I was a funny, sad child, an introverted extrovert. Someone once told me my inner child was an adult, and I thought that was spot-on! It also implies my outer adult is a child...

TWR   I think that perhaps I meant some of your pieces in *My Private Property* (the girl who salts her friend's milkshake while she's in the bathroom, for instance). But also several of your poems take place in classrooms, or make reference to specific grades or ages (ones that spring to mind here are 'Provenance', 'Middle School', 'The Hand'). I think also the sense of seeing things afresh, for the first time, that comes with reading a lot of your work, feels somehow equivalent to the gaze of a child. A poem of yours I particularly love is 'Nice Hands', which feels to me like it encapsulates the utter weirdness of being born and having to grow up in the world.
MR   Thank you. As I age, memories of my early/earlier years come flooding back to me, it's quite strange but many people my own age have had the same experience; things you have not thought of or remembered in years come back to you. 'Provenance' is true to my experience, that papier-maché horse I made was one of my first works of 'art' and we really did have to give our animals, as a class, to the girl who was dying in hospital... After I wrote the poem, after it was published, I remembered that I had not in fact named the horse Aurora, but Arabella... The other poems you mention are not particularly rooted in my childhood, with the possible exception of 'Nice Hands', in which the kittens appear... That really was how I pictured my stomach when I was little, and I later found the book with the picture in it

that gave rise to this insane fantasy of mine, it's one of those books where they put clothes on real kittens and photograph them in different situations. I must have seen that, as a child. It *is* weird, being a child; you have a picture of the world that is very different than the one you have as a grown-up. We all love children for that.

TWR   Another 'neglected' process you're interested in is the menopause. In 'Pause', you include a scan of a handwritten inventory taken while you were undergoing the menopause – this 'Crylog' tallies each day, recording the number of times you cried during the month of April. On reflection though, the speaker finds her own pain faintly ridiculous. To look at it in retrospect makes her laugh. Again, in the book's Acknowledgments you suggest that in each of the 'colour' pieces, 'if you substitute the word happiness for the word sadness, nothing changes'. Do you see a certain intimacy between suffering and humour? (I often find my suffering ridiculous in its aftermath.)
MR   No, I don't find suffering humorous; there is nothing funny about not having enough to eat, or losing your child in a bombing, or any number of other horrible examples of sufferings we find on earth, many of them preventable. But I do find it funny when someone acts like they are suffering when the electricity goes off for a few hours, or they have to wait in a queue at the post office. At the same time, isn't it wrong to evaluate or judge another's sufferings? When a child drops an ice cream cone in the grass and wails, her suffering fills her whole world at that moment, she has lost her beloved no less than the widow. It is only as we grow and change that we are able to evaluate and judge our own suffering, and never that of another. To grow and change and put our sufferings into perspective – that is the challenge. It doesn't diminish them, but it may prevent many from reoccurring, I mean those that are the result of our own tiny twisted minds.

   I think when you ask if there is an intimacy between suffering and humour you may mean suffering and joy, and certainly there is an intimacy between them as we define each as the absence of the other, not to mention they are inseparable parts of life, as the joy of birth *guarantees* the suffering of death. Shakespeare wrote comedies as well as tragedies. There is no literature as we know it without an intimacy between the two.

TWR   It's like in 'New Morning' where the speaker's experience of tasting soured cream in her coffee is framed as an 'unbearable' form of suffering. The poem is so funny in part because the speaker's suffering appears laughable. But, at the time, the taste of spoiled milk *is* truly disgusting, verging on insufferable. From an external perspective, it's ridiculous; but also drinking it is definitely an experience you wouldn't want to repeat.
MR   That is true; minor sufferings can, at the moment they occur, fill our whole world (or mouth!) but hopefully one stops and puts them in perspective. When a dish breaks in my house, I call out 'Good Luck!' – meaning that it brings good luck, to have something broken. I would never call that out if a tree fell on my house, destroying the roof...

TWR   There is a dark humour in a lot of your poems. I was re-reading *The Most of It* the other day and found myself laughing at a line in 'Snow' – 'It is snowing and I must go have sex, good-bye'. Do you set out to be funny in your work?
MR   Oh no, I never set out to be funny, 'Snow' was not supposed to be funny, and ultimately isn't, but I *do* have a sense of humour and it invariably sets in, even if it ends in grief. I never reread my own work, but I had to when my *Selected Poems* was in production, and I found myself laughing, I simply could not believe how funny many of the poems were. Maybe all my poems are written out of ridiculous grief – like sour milk – and I only later find it laughable. Wait, that's not true, there *are* times I set out humorously, only to take a turn later; I guess I am a serious, sad person with a terrific sense of humour. A sense of humour can save you, you know. It can save you from doing terrible things like putting a gun to your head.

TWR   The Crylog made me think about the actual liquidity of tears, and the sheer volume that must be shed by each of us across the course of our lives. I wonder, if collected, what size container would be needed to hold them.
MR   Don't you know the oceans contain all the tears ever shed by anyone who ever lived? The Pacific, the Atlantic, and all the seas combined – all the tears, which evaporate and form clouds from which rain falls, watering the crops we eat with joy.

TWR   You have an essay 'On Sentimentality'
in *Madness, Rack, and Honey*. Do you still consider
yourself 'a sentimental poet'? What do you feel is
the place of sentimentality in poetry now?
MR   Oh yes, I feel I am still a sentimental
poet, and that all poets are sentimental, even if
they hate sentimentality; as I said in that essay, to
write a poem is a sentimental act in the first place.
I may not be considered or seen as a sentimental
poet, but, like the others, I am, I am. Neruda said:
'He who flees from sentimentality flees from
poetry itself.'

TWR   In 'Pause' ageing starts out as a form
of violence – a cause for despair or, more starkly,
ending one's own life. The woman feels herself
to have lost total control of her body, and of the
way it's assessed by others. This culminates in a
complex form of erasure that is sadly common to
the lived experience of many older women – 'others
look straight through you, you are completely
invisible to them, you have become a ghost'. It
also, conflictingly, precipitates a renewed desire
for visibility, that you suggest results in peculiar
exhibitionist behaviours. But, ultimately, this
age-induced invisibility is revealed as something
liberating – 'the biggest secret on earth, the most
wondrous gift anyone could ever have given you'.
What do you mean by this? And how does this
secret knowledge become compatible with the
pain endured to access it?
MR   I think it is difficult to tell a young woman
that her inevitable 'invisibility' will become a great
joy; you are young, and you want me to explain
how that can be so, but I would much rather have
you experience it yourself, and so all I can do is put
my hand on your shoulder and express a wish that
you stay out of harm's way and live long enough to
come to know and understand it yourself, in your
bones, on the touchstone of your heart. I suppose
that is a sentimental answer, but what good would
such knowledge do you now? Like Rilke said, your
job is to 'live the questions' now, so that in the far
future you may live your way into the answers.

C. T.,
January 2019

SWINE

ARIANA HARWICZ
tr. ANNIE McDERMOTT
& CAROLINA ORLOFF

1.

From outside the Necker Hospital, I saw him run up the stairs and through the rooms of deformed babies. When he shouted in my ear in a noisy Paris bar that he was having a child with another woman, that it was an accident, we weren't yet us, I hadn't even touched him. My life was bourgeois, almost monogamous. After the birth, I went to his house and found him barbecuing sausages on a crumbling concrete patio. The baby hadn't yet been diagnosed but already it was crying too much, choking itself. I saw their clothes in the hallway, coats hanging up, ski boots piled in the porch, envelopes and papers with their names side by side. Nothing suggested he could kill a dog and leave its mangled body in a ditch, not his neatly ironed clothes, his collars and combs, the suitcases he shared with his wife. He hadn't smashed any windows, he hadn't yet crashed; there were no shredded clothes, no bleeding backsides, no massacre laid at my door. We walked through the hanging garden in the hospital, our hands not yet clasped, our tongues not yet tasted, our eyes still in their sockets. Remembering this now is like fishing turtles out of the water by their necks. The babies cried, bewildered, unable to suckle. Like puppies. One baby in each dark little room. One baby in each box like a sinister surprise. I marked that day in the calendar to show when the fever took hold. Passion always emerges from the depths, like sea monsters.

2.

Death can exist in an empty bottle tossed onto the subway tracks, in an umbrella stand, in a Roman bridge over a high ravine. Ours was a passion like Anna Akhmatova's, seventeen months exactly without moving an inch from the queue outside the Leningrad prisons, longing to see her captured lover. But Stalin never gave him back. She hanged herself right there and a street cleaner had to take her down and sweep her away. Stories of passion need to be told, even in someone else's words. Words always come from someone else. We talk and then we die without having said anything.

3.

Our first kiss was the first time we saw each other with the sky unlit. We had dinner in a café on the Rue Oberkampf and some passing Arabs yelled for him to propose. We're already married, we explained. But I can love two men at once / But I can love two women at the same time, we said. First we reached one another through glasses of wine. There was already a history, of us meeting at a wedding, of us having danced, tall as we were, glittering as we were in the crystals, in a stroll by the lakeside like a portrait, in the skylights. And the first kiss with no witnesses in that bar, because places don't exist, lights don't exist, and his wife on the phone berating him when we left, the first signs of discord, the defeated delusional rhetoric of jealousy. Me sprawled on the pavement and his wife saying we were whispering words like flames and him saying not at all, whatever gave her that idea, he'd been working at the ambulance depot; denying my existence before my very eyes whilst gazing at me wild with desire. The Paris tow truck had taken his car. Riding in a taxi on that September night, lost who knows where, a taxi carrying us flying to the graveyard of badly parked cars. A taxi that sends us soaring to perdition. He paid in the traffic office, money through the bars. I want you, he cried, I want you, like a caged animal. I want you, I want you, but he hadn't yet lost his mind. Then he drove all the way back at full speed. Scalded. Nameless. Not stopping at the lights, ignoring the street signs, and that's when he flattened a black dog that was limping down the road. The dog flew into the ditch but he carried on, with nothing ahead but the sky ripping in half.

4.

Hoche Avenue. Royal Monceau. He hadn't seen me but we were there, both of us. The first untenable step into the lobby. The lift attacked by two rowdy Americans, sullying my excitement. I walked towards the main staircase. The old men watching, knowing what they've lost, ageing granddads sniffing other people's passion under lecherous hotel doors. *Chambre 1311*. Four hours later this place will no longer exist. It will burn. One last look at the chandeliers, the oil paintings. My eyes hanging from his. Compulsion. Coming at his heart over my head. He was mine. Travelling thousands of miles to have that heart. The lahar in an active volcano. Like the night-terror screams after a school bus crashes.

5.

The marks of our hands on the wallpaper. We spent hours like that, switching the lights on and burning them out. This is passion, I said in a German bathtub, like a chant in a foreign language, like a motorbike ride down wild country roads. My wife heard your name last night in my sleep, but I was mumbling away in your Spanish and she didn't understand a thing. He put his boots on and went out to burn bushes that weren't meant to be destroyed, and he almost set fire to the house, the cat, the dog, his daughter in her highchair and his wife. And all those hours switching rooms beds bodies. The towering ghost of the Alhambra at night. A grave under tangled stems and soil like a homicidal passion. We were born without lips and they came when we kissed. Madrid, London, Berlin, Prague, Bruges, Valencia, Granada, Giverny, Crouzon, Le Mont St Michel, Honfleur, Deauville, Tréauville and back to Madrid. I wondered what would happen if he found out where I am, here, now, as they try to revive me. That was the scene. He would learn about my death, about the four hours spent fighting to bring me back. And that would be me, gone, never knowing what he'd said, what he'd done in the hour after hearing the news, the night after, that summer, the first Christmas. I would die having completely lost my mind.

6.

Jealousy is a child marked out for use in experiments, lying there naked, eyes injected with typhus. Jealousy is white cows and an idiot farmer trying to make them graze. Shake off desire and have time to be. Shake off desire and let your lungs breathe. The way a mystic stretches out on the tiles to cool down and levitate but can't because he's erect. Desire is always there like a cliff edge. Wherever you go, men were always sucked off, in the hills, in the Pyramids, in the Roman circus, their brains gulped down too for good measure. You're not picking up, where are you? I bequeath you my dirtiest, most maddening thoughts, my most sacred incantations. Call me. Right now while I wait, while I'm dying even after I'm dead.

7.

I am the soul of Caesar in a woman's body. I crash against the fence but see no blood. You're not picking up. You've disappeared. How many times was the door ajar and I didn't notice. How many times did the sky of the free shine outside, there for the taking, there for me to sink myself in the inner workings of the motorway and become a traveller or a beggar. Desire is pathetic. Not even I can face myself. I'm a fanatic, a joke. Are you not here yet? I see your shadow in the house and chase it through the rooms, I float along embracing it, raping it. He was breathing a murderer's air and he didn't realise. I didn't realise either. Funny that. Now I'm coming to find you. You'll be the swine with its brains blown out.

8.

Now the beast is gone, remembering its body is impossible, is lacerating. It's a seizure wrongly treated with morphine, an overdose, joining a dying man as he strolls one last time through the park. A tomb. I won't say a thing about his body or mine. I'll leave it there in the kingdom of hell and Kalashnikov attacks. In that hell of morbid lies, aflame and unhinged. I'll say nothing, give nothing away. There was no penetration swathed in glamour, elegance and knee-high stockings, no fingers slid into the ass through black lace, no ejaculations like an army's thick red gunfire over the Thames. There were no sparks in the clitoris or potions in the veins for sixteen hours until the ambulance. There was no afternoon in Pigalle, his body and mine, my body and his, unthinkable unthinking masturbating the eyes in the tongues of twenty languages. There was no room fucked to smithereens or lust savage enough to bury us in Montparnasse. It wasn't love. Love is nothing, love is for everyone. Love is possible.

APPENDIX

KHAIRANI BAROKKA is an Indonesian writer, poet and artist in London whose work has been presented extensively, in thirteen countries. She is the writer, performer and producer of hearing-impaired accessible solo show *Eve and Mary Are Having Coffee*, author-illustrator of *Indigenous Species* (Tilted Axis, 2017), and author of poetry collection *Rope* (Nine Arches, 2017). Her latest art installation was *Annah: Nomenclature* at the ICA. She is a Visual Cultures PhD researcher at Goldsmiths, and *Modern Poetry in Translation*'s inaugural Poet/Translator in Residence.

RENATE BERTLMANN (b. 1943, Vienna, Austria) has been working at the heart of feminist art since the late 1960s. Her diverse practice spans painting, drawing, collage, photography, sculpture and performance, and actively confronts the social stereotypes assigned to masculine and feminine behaviours and relationships. Her work has been included in many important institutional exhibitions around the world, and she will be the first woman to be the sole representative of the Austrian Pavilion at the Venice Biennale, opening in May 2019.

RAHUL BERY is a translator from Spanish and Portuguese into English, based in Cardiff. His translations have appeared in *Granta*, *The White Review*, *Words Without Borders* and *Latin American Literature Today*, among others. He is currently Translator in Residence at the British Library.

KATE BRIGGS is a writer and translator based in Rotterdam. She is the translator of two volumes of Roland Barthes's lecture notes at the Collège de France, an experience which informed *This Little Art* (Fitzcarraldo Editions, 2017), a long essay on the practice of literary translation. Recent work includes 'I am a Live Creature! Form as Experience', a lecture delivered at Glasgow International (2018), 'Of the Novel Experimental', a partial retranslation of Emile Zola's *Le roman expérimental* published in *Do Not Make The* (MAP, 2018), and 'Entertaining Ideas', a short essay on writing backwards forthcoming from Ma Bibliothèque. She teaches at the Piet Zwart Institute, Rotterdam.

HEATHER CHRISTLE is the author of four poetry collections, most recently *Heliopause*. Her first work of non-fiction, *The Crying Book*, will be out in the UK in early 2020.

THEODORA DANEK is the publisher of Tilted Axis Press and edits *PEN Transmissions*. She is based in Vienna, Austria.

NAEL ELTOUKHY is an Egyptian novelist, essayist, journalist and translator of Hebrew literature into Arabic, who currently lives in Berlin. He has published two novellas and three novels in Arabic. The English translation of his second novel, *Women of Karantina* (AUC Press, 2014), was shortlisted for the fiction prize of the 2015 FT/OppenheimerFunds Emerging Voices Awards. His most recent novel, *Out of the Gutter*, which is extracted here, was published in Arabic in 2018.

ANTHEA HAMILTON (b. 1978, London) is based in London. She was one of four shortlisted artists for the 2016 Turner Prize. Her recent solo shows include: *The New Life*, Secession, Vienna, *The Squash*, Tate Britain, London; *Anthea Hamilton Reimagines Kettle's Yard*, Hepworth Wakefield, UK; *LICHEN! LIBIDO! CHASTITY!* at SculptureCenter, New York; *Sorry I'm Late*, Firstsite, Colchester, UK; *Les Modules*, Foundation Pierre Berge – Yves Saint Laurent, Palais de Tokyo, Paris. Her work has been presented as part of the British Art Show 8 and in numerous international venues, such as at the Schinkel Pavillon, Berlin (with Nicholas Byrne), the 13th Lyon Biennale and the 10th Gwangju Biennale.

ARIANA HARWICZ (b. Buenos Aires, 1977) is one of the most radical figures in contemporary Argentinian literature. Harwicz studied screenwriting and drama in Argentina, and earned a first degree in Performing Arts from the University of Paris VII as well as a Master's degree in comparative literature from the Sorbonne. *Feebleminded* (published by Charco Press in May 2019) is her second novel and the second instalment of an 'involuntary' trilogy, preceded by *Die, My Love* (Charco Press, 2017) and followed by *Precoz* [Precocious, 2015]. Her fourth novel is *Degenerado* [Degenerate], which came out in Spanish in January 2019.

SANYA KANTAROVSKY's (b. 1980, Russia) recent exhibitions include solo presentations at Kunsthalle Basel, Switzerland and Fondazione Sandretto Re Rebaudengo, Turin, Italy; group shows at Jewish Museum, New York and Sculpture Center, New York; as well as his curatorial project

Sputterances at Metro Pictures, New York. A comprehensive monograph entitled *No Joke* was co-published by Studio Voltaire and Koenig Books in 2016. His works belong to prestigious museum collections including Hirshhorn Museum and Sculpture Garden, Washington D.C.; Institute of Contemporary Art/Boston; Hammer Museum, Los Angeles; Los Angeles County Museum of Art; Tate Modern, London; and Whitney Museum of American Art, New York. He currently lives and works in New York.

EMILY LABARGE is a Canadian writer living in London, where she teaches at the Royal College of Art. Amongst other publications, she has written for *Frieze*, *Tate Etc.*, *LA Review of Books*, *Bookforum*, and the *Guardian*.

KAREN McCARTHY WOOLF was born in London to English and Jamaican parents. She holds a Prairie Schooner Glenna Luschei Editors' Prize and this year was awarded residencies at Hedgebrook and Ucross in the US. She also writes essays, drama and documentary for BBC radios 3 and 4 and her work has been translated into Spanish, Turkish and Swedish. Her latest collection is *Seasonal Disturbances* (Carcanet, 2017).

ANNIE McDERMOTT translates fiction and poetry from Spanish and Portuguese. Her translations of *Empty Words* and *The Luminous Novel*, by the Uruguayan writer Mario Levrero, are forthcoming from And Other Stories and Coffee House Press, and her co-translation of *City of Ulysses* by Teolinda Gersão (with Jethro Soutar) was published by Dalkey Archive Press in 2017.

ROBIN MOGER is a translator of contemporary Arabic literature, based in Cape Town.

CAROLINA ORLOFF is an experienced translator and researcher in Latin American literature, who has published extensively on the writer Julio Cortázar as well as on literature, cinema, politics and translation theory. In 2016, after obtaining her PhD and working in the academic sector for several years, Carolina co-founded Charco Press where she acts as publishing director and main editor. She is also the co-translator of Ariana Harwicz's *Die, My Love*, which was longlisted for the Man Booker International Prize 2018 and shortlisted for the Republic of Consciousness Prize. Originally from Buenos Aires, she is now based in Edinburgh.

NJ STALLARD is a writer, editor and poet. Her work has been featured in publications such as *Tank*, *Broadly*, *Ambit*, *Hotel* and *PN Review*, and she was the winner of the Aleph Writing Prize 2018. She is working on her first novel.

JAKOB STOUGAARD-NIELSEN is Associate Professor in Scandinavian Literature at UCL. He has recently completed a collaborative research project on Translating the Literatures from Small European Nations, funded by the Arts and Humanities Research Council.

REBECCA TAMÁS is a Lecturer in Creative Writing at York St John University. Her pamphlet *Savage* was published by Clinic Press, and was a LRB Bookshop pamphlet of the year, and a Poetry School book of the year. She is editor, with Sarah Shin, of *Spells: 21st Century Occult Poetry*, published by Ignota Books. Rebecca's first full-length poetry collection, *WITCH*, will be published by Penned in the Margins in March 2019.

ADAM THIRLWELL has written three novels, *Politics*, *The Escape*, and *Lurid & Cute*; edited a project with international novelists called *Multiples*; and, most recently, written and directed a short film called *Utopia*. His work is translated into thirty languages.

CECILIA TRICKER is a PhD candidate working between the English department at Sheffield University, and the Department of Philosophy and Theology at Leeds. She is Online Editor at *The White Review*.

ZAKIA UDDIN lives in East London. She has written for *The Wire* and other publications, including *Paris Review Daily* and the *LRB* blog.

ALEJANDRO ZAMBRA has published *Bonsai*, *The Private Lives of Trees*, *Ways of Going Home*, *My Documents*, *Multiple Choice* and *Not to Read*, among other books. His work is translated into twenty languages.

PLATES

ON TRANSLATION

Ahmed, Sara, 'feministkilljoys', <https://feministkilljoys.com>

Atkin, Rhian, Rajendra Chitnis, Jakob Stougaard-Nielsen and Zoran Milutinović, 'Translating the Literatures of Small European Nations' (2014-2016), <http://www.bristol.ac.uk/arts/research/translating-sen>

Barokka, Khairani, *Indigenous Species* (Sheffield: Tilted Axis Press, 2016)

    'money for your english'. In *Asian American Writers' Workshop's Transpacific Literary Project, The Margins, ASEAN at 50: Poems from Across Southeast Asia,* <https://aaww.org/asean-at-50-poems-from-across-southeast-asia/>

    'Translation of/as Absence, Sanctuary, Weapon', *Poetry Review*, 108:2 (2018), <http://poetrysociety.org.uk/translation-of-as-absence>

Bertolotti-Bailey, Francesca, Stuart Bertolotti-Bailey, Vincenzo Latronico, David Reinfurt, eds, *The Serving Library Annual 2018/19: Translation* (Amsterdam: Roma Publications, 2018)

Briggs, Kate, *This Little Art* (London: Fitzcarraldo Editions, 2017)

Calleja, Jen, 'Attempts by the Alchemists', *Brixton Review of Books*, 2018

Carson, Ciaran, Introduction, in *The Inferno Of Dante Alighieri* (London: Granta, 2002)

Collins, Sophie, 'Erasing the signs of labour under the signs of happiness: "joy" and "fidelity" as bromides in literary translation', *Poetry Review*, 108:2 (2018), <http://poetrysociety.org.uk/erasing-the-signs-of-labour>

    Currently and Emotion: Translations (Norwich: Test Centre, 2016)

Dodson, Katrina, 'Understanding is the Proof of Error', *The Believer*, 11 July 2018, <https://believermag.com/understanding-is-the-proof-of-error/>

Mehrotra, Arvind Krishna, Introduction, in *Songs of Kabir* (New York: NYRB Classics, 2011)

Rosenwald, Lawrence, '"New language fun", or, on translating multilingual American texts', *Multilingual America* (Cambridge: Cambridge University Press, 2008), pp.122-145

Shanbhag, Vivvek, *Ghachar Ghochar*, tr. by Srinath Perur (London: Faber & Faber, 2017)

Smith, Deborah, 'What We Talk About When We Talk About Translation', *Los Angeles Review of Books*, 11 January 2018, <https://lareviewofbooks.org/article/what-we-talk-about-when-we-talk-about-translation/>

'Translating Feminism: Transfer, Transgression, Transformation (1945-Present)', <https://translatingfeminism.org>

Venuti, Lawrence, *The Translator's Invisibility: A History of Translation* (London: Routledge, 2008)

Wilson, Emily, Introduction, in *The Odyssey* (London: W.W. Norton & Company, 2017)

    '@EmilyRCWilson Scholia', <https://www.emilyrcwilson.com/emilyrcwilson-scholia>

Kate Murphy

13 April to 12 May

BANK

1 June to 7 July

Piper Keys
Exhibitions

Supported using public funding by
ARTS COUNCIL
ENGLAND
LOTTERY FUNDED

www.piperkeys.com

Bluecoat

A season of exhibitions exploring the changing nature of artistic education.

The Art Schools of North West England
John Beck & Matthew Cornford

Instituting Care
Jade Montserrat

Studio Me
Joshua Henderson & Veronica Watson

Until Sun 31 Mar 2019

www.thebluecoat.org.uk
🐦 @thebluecoat 📷 @the_bluecoat f @thebluecoat

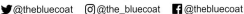
Liverpool City Council   Supported using public funding by ARTS COUNCIL ENGLAND   The Granada Foundation   University of Brighton   UNIVERSITY OF WESTMINSTER

Jade Montserrat, *The Last Place They Thought Of*, Installation View, Institute of Contemporary Art, University of Pennsylvania. Photo: Constance Mensh

CHANGE
YOUR MIND

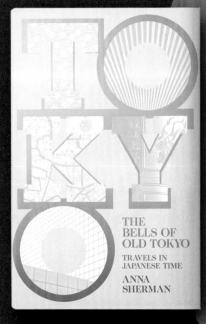

THE
BELLS OF
OLD TOKYO

TRAVELS IN
JAPANESE TIME

ANNA
SHERMAN

Paul takes
the form of
a mortal girl
Andrea Lawlor

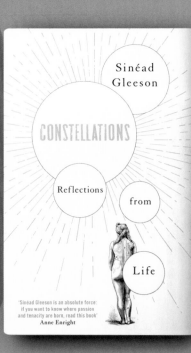

Sinéad
Gleeson

CONSTELLATIONS

Reflections · from

Life

'Sinéad Gleeson is an absolute force:
if you want to know where passion
and tenacity are born, read this book'
Anne Enright

Fresh new voices from

The extraordinary debut collection from
White Review Short Story Prize winner

NICOLE FLATTERY

'I truly love and admire Nicole Flattery's writing. *Show Them a Good Time* is a masterclass in the short story – bold, irreverent and agonisingly funny – and it does full justice to its author's immense talent'

SALLY ROONEY

BLOOMSBURY

PhD in Creative Writing

Full-time or part-time | September entry

Our practice-based programme is for committed writers of fiction, poetry, and creative non-fiction. We will help you complete a book-length creative project while preparing you for a long-term career in writing.

You will benefit from:

- **Regular feedback sessions** with your thesis supervisor
- **Termly workshops** with your peers
- **Literary agents-in-residence** offering one-to-one meetings
- **Advice and practical insights** from guest authors, editors, and publishers
- **Teaching undergraduate writers** through our Graduate Teaching Assistantship scheme
- **Curating literary events**, including our *Poetry And...* series

Our teaching team currently features prize-winning novelists, poets, and creative non-fiction specialists: **Ruth Padel**, **Benjamin Wood**, **Edmund Gordon**, **Jon Day**, **Lara Feigel**, **Sarah Howe**, and **Andrew O'Hagan** (Visiting Research Fellow).

FACULTY OF ARTS & HUMANITIES **FIND OUT MORE AT KCL.AC.UK/STUDY**